Misguided Justice

A BEACH MURDER MYSTERY

Bascom Wilson

Misguided Justice
by Bascom Wilson

© Copyright 2011 by Bascom Wilson

ISBN 978-1-938467-12-7

A BEACH MURDER MYSTERY BOOK
www.beachmurdermysteries.com

Published by
köehlerbooks™
an imprint of Morgan James Publishing

5 Penn Plaza, 23rd floor
c/o Morgan James Publishing
New York, NY 10001
212-574-7939
www.koehlerbooks.com

Publisher
John Köehler

Executive Editor
Joe Coccaro

  In an effort to support local communities, raise awareness and funds, Morgan James Publishing donates a percentage of all book sales for the life of each book to Habitat for Humanity Peninsula and Greater Williamsburg.
Get involved today, visit www.MorganJamesBuilds.com

Misguided Justice

Bascom Wilson

NEW YORK

VIRGINIA

Thanks to all who supported me
in this adventure. I want to
especially thank my wife, Nina,
for encouraging me to proceed.
Without a dream, there is no progress.

1

Slumped behind tall dune grass, he watches the bikini-clad woman bask in summer's warmth. She seems relaxed, lounging in a wooden chair with an e-tablet. She cranes her head back and closes her eyes, absorbing the sun and serenity of this remote patch of Chesapeake Bay beach. She's alone with no one else in sight. White sand frames her lean, bronze figure. An umbrella blocks the Bay breeze, but not the view through his binoculars. He studies her, breathing lightly and crouching motionless like a deer hunter in a tree stand. The notorious and ruthless female attorney from New York City doesn't look so ruthless now, he thinks. In fact, she looks sensual and vulnerable.

Newspaper articles hailed her as the youngest

partner in one of New York City's largest law firms. She had landed the firm's biggest client and was rewarded by being named a partner in the firm. Thinking about the attention she received, about the fawning from others in the firm, agitates him. That much recognition and reward were undeserved. Others were passed over, others who had toiled longer and remained loyal. Her looks, youth, and gender got her ahead; not skill or brains. To calm himself, he focuses on his mission.

His heart pounds as the moment nears. A flock of screeching seagulls swoop in just as he starts his approach. Their screeching and squawking provide a cover. This must be an omen—the sign he needs. She looks peaceful, strewn in the chair with eyes closed. He stands next to her for a few seconds, admiring her toned body and flawless skin. So beautiful, he thinks. What a waste! He can't dawdle for fear of being seen by the late-afternoon beach walkers. But he wants her to see her killer and for her to seize with fear. "Wake up! Wake up, you arrogant bitch," he shouts. Still in a sleepy haze, her blue eyes blink and then focus on the familiar face. She gasps at the metallic gun pointing at her head—her last breath.

2

Jack Sinclair procrastinated, catching the last ferry returning from Tangier Island. He arrives home early this Sunday morning groggy, but knowing he has all day to rest from his weekend trip. He pulls off his clothes and tosses them into the hamper by the closet. Within a couple of minutes, he's asleep.

He had just dozed off when jarred awake by a ringing noise. With his eyes closed, he reaches for the cell phone on the nightstand. Who the hell would be calling me so early on a Sunday morning!?! he thinks. He becomes even more agitated as he clumsily fumbles around for the phone in the dark. "This had better be important," he tells the caller. "Don't you know it's Sunday!?! "

"Where in the hell have you been? You alone?" asks the voice on the other end.

Jack recognizes the voice as Dan Miller, Onancock's police lieutenant and a childhood friend. He says, "Hell no, I'm not alone! I'm with the Willard twins, you idiot! What's up?" He knows this will raise Dan's temperature, since Dan married one of the Willard twins about five years ago.

"We have a crime scene. So get your hand off your dick and get your ass out of the bed now," Dan says.

"Who the hell requested me so damn early?"

"Randy" says Dan. That's all Dan needed to say to rouse Jack. Jack knew that if Randy Walker, Onancock's medical examiner, requested him at the crime scene it had to be important.

"OK, text me the location. I'm out in twenty," Jack says.

"You had better make it in ten if you don't want Randy busting your balls," laughs Dan as he clicks off his cell.

Jack rolls out of bed and heads to the shower. Being that Jack is a former Marine, he knows the importance of showering quickly. He grabs a clean shirt and jeans. Slacks are too businesslike for him. Polo shirts and jeans or shorts are his preferred dress code. He had been hassled about his less-than professional attire when he first started with the OPD, but being that he was the only detective for the northern section of Virginia's Eastern Shore, his captain let him slide.

Jack removes his gun from the locked safe, located on his closet shelf, along with a newly loaded magazine, and then heads for the door. It's still dark outside. He checks the text message for the location of the crime scene. He reads the address twice before it finally hits him; it's only two blocks away. When he left Washington, DC and decided to return to the Eastern Shore, he invested the money he had received from the sale of his Herndon, Virginia home for a beachfront bungalow. He had always wanted to live in one of the elegant homes on the Chesapeake Bay. The only downfall is its proximity to Onancock's beach rental district.

After viewing the text message, he climbs into his 2009 Jaguar XKR convertible and heads for the crime scene. A bachelor, Jack loves his cars like he loves his women—fast, furious, and elegant.

When he arrives at the scene, Jerry O'Sullivan, one of the new rookie officers, greets him at the curb in front of the house. Jack knows all the new rookies by their first names. It makes them feel integral to the team. As a former Marine officer, he made it a habit to learn the names of everyone in his platoon. He continued this practice when he left the Marines and joined the police force.

"Hey, Jerry! Do you know why I was called?" asks Jack.

"Detective Sinclair, we have a body on the beach. The medical examiner is here and asked for you specifically. I was told to wait here until you arrived."

"OK, I'm here, so lead the way!" Jack says with a smile.

The rookie escorts him onto a beach access path, which is nothing more than a three-foot wide sandy path with a broken fence on both sides. The path starts near tourist rental houses and winds over a short dune and onto the beach. Bay beaches tend to be narrower than sprawling oceanfront, umbrella-strewn resorts such as the Jersey Shore or Virginia Beach, which is about an hour and a half drive south across the Chesapeake Bay. The Eastern Shore is dotted with small farm towns, often of just a few hundred residents, snaking farm roads and historic villages. Onancock is metropolitan by comparison to most, boasting two large discount department stores, a high school, its own police department, art galleries, and some fine dining. History buffs flock here; the town dates to 1680 and is known for its snazzy Victorian inns. Violent crime here seems incongruous.

As Jack approaches the murder scene, he greets the medical examiner. "Good morning, Randy, haven't seen you in a while. I hear that you missed me!" Jack chuckles.

Kneeling next to the body, Randy turns and looks at Jack with a grimace. Randy is accustomed to Jack's sarcasm and always expects it.

Randy had practiced as a general family practitioner directly after he finished his internship at George Washington University Hospital in Washington, DC. During his residency, he decided that he had had enough of the big city hospitals. He returned to Onancock to follow in his father's footsteps, a door-to-door country doctor. When he turned forty, he quit treating the living for his current job of examining the dead. Now in his mid-sixties, he maintains the same sense of sarcasm as he had when he was younger.

"Yep, missed you terribly! Where you've been lately? I haven't slept a single hour since our last encounter!" Randy quips.

Jack looks at the rookie and sees that he is blushing. "It's OK, we are only kidding each other. Can you go and get some information from the neighbors?" The rookie turns and walks toward the beach path.

"Randy, you have to be careful around these new rookies. They are so impressionable."

"And you aren't?" asks Randy.

"OK, so, what do we have?" asks Jack.

"Preliminary finding is that this young woman was sleeping on the beach. It appears that she had awakened long enough to see her attacker when she was shot. You can see what we call 'the shock in her eyes'."

"Got a time of death, yet?" Jack could be a little anxious to get information. He developed a keen sense over the years of reading crime scenes. Randy also knows this about Jack and is careful not to disclose too much right away.

"Got any insights yet?" prods Randy. "I can only estimate the time of death as sometime between eight and ten o'clock last night."

"What? Why are we just now being called? What took so long?" asks Jack.

Randy ignores Jack's comment and continues. "The call came in around five this morning from the neighbors staying next door. They had just walked onto the beach for their morning jog when they saw her still laying here on the sunbed. The female neighbor had remembered seeing this woman around six last evening when she and her husband had left the beach for their own house. When they saw her this morning, they thought she had just fallen asleep and slept in the sun chair all night. They were going to awaken her, when they saw all of the blood. That was when they called 9-1-1."

Jack looked around the beach toward the neighbors' house and then turned back to Randy as he continued.

"There are two gunshot wounds to the body, one to the head and another to the heart. It will be hard to determine which one was the fatal shot since they both seem to have been done within a few seconds of each other. My prediction, at this time, is that the shot to the head was an afterthought. I will know better once I get her back to the morgue. There appears to be no signs of a struggle."

Just as Randy concludes, Jerry, the rookie patrolman, taps Jack on the shoulder. This startles him. He had not seen nor heard Jerry return.

"Damn, Jerry, you scared the shit out of me."

"Sorry, I thought you heard me. The neighbors

would like to talk to you," he says. "They asked who was in charge and I said you were. They said that they have some information they would like to share with you." Jack excuses himself from Randy and follows the rookie to the waiting neighbors.

Jack extends his hand and shakes each of theirs. "Good morning. Detective Sinclair. You asked to speak with me?"

"Yes, we are Mary and Jonathon Wilcox. We are renting the house next door. We met the young lady a couple of days ago when she first arrived. She said her name was Janet Hastings, an attorney from New York City." Mary talks so fast that Jack asks her to slow down a bit. Mary continues: "She said she was here for a vacation. Who could have done this? Do you think we are safe here? Should we end our vacation and leave?"

Jack consoles the neighbors, telling them they will be safe. He says that Jerry will need a written statement from them. He thanks them for the information and watches Jerry accompany the neighbors toward their house.

Jack notices the crime scene unit starting to arrive. This would be a good time for him to exit, so he turns and heads for the same beach path he had used earlier, this time to exit the beach. It was time for the

CSU team to gather its evidence. He was sure that the team would get its preliminary reports later this morning. He would make time to meet with Randy later as well.

A former Marine sniper and an ex-Washington, DC police detective, Jack left the big city life for the peaceful small town community life of Onancock. He was raised on the small town life of the Eastern Shore of Virginia. He had accepted the position of the only detective for the Onancock police force and later became the only major crime unit detective for the entire northern portion of the Eastern Shore of Virginia. He has held this position for the better part of five years without seeing a single major crime. Today, that statistic changed.

"What a fuckin' way to start the day!" he mutters while walking toward his car.

3

He wanted to hide in the dune grass on the beach and watch how the Keystone Kops in this backwater town of fifteen hundred residents would handle what he had done; but he also knew that staying could get him caught. He had no remorse. In his mind, she deserved to die. It was about self-preservation.

He left the beach later than he had planned. He had imagined how the night's full moon would glisten over the calm waters of the Bay as he returned to the room he had rented at a local historic bed and breakfast, The Inn at Onancock. Squatting on the beach behind the dune grass for hours left him stiff and sore. When he finally entered his room at The Inn he pulled off his clothes and tossed them in a corner. The soft pillowtop mattress was going to be a godsend.

After just a few hours of sleep, he was awakened to the smell of freshly baked biscuits, blueberry pancakes, and freshly brewed coffee. The smells of the early breakfast resonated throughout the upper rooms of the B&B. He could definitely tell that he was in the South. Freshly baked biscuits had to be the norm for the early morning risers in the Southern states.

He rolled out of the overly stuffed bed and headed for the shower. He dressed and packed and then he headed downstairs for breakfast before checking out. He was just another traveler enjoying the sights of the Eastern Shore.

As he sat in the small dining area sipping his coffee and waiting for his order of blueberry pancakes, he knew he had a long drive north back to the city. But he still had another task to complete.

The waitress arrived with his breakfast and a smile. All was good.

4

The Onancock Police Department was established in the 1930s in a small warehouse that was left vacant from the early fishing days of Onancock. The OPD subdivided the space with administrative offices, a squad room, one interrogation room, and an area that housed three cells. In the early days, the cells were only used for the occasional drunk or bar brawlers. Even though the building fit OPD's needs and budget, it still reminded the police officers that they worked in a fishing warehouse.

In April 2006, the OPD expanded with a major crime unit. The new unit was created to investigate all the major crimes from the central Eastern Shore to the Maryland border. With the incorporation of this

new squad, the OPD had to find a new location to ex-
pand. The town council approved a new police station
within the tourist shopping area. The building would
be designed to match surrounding historic buildings,
to blend in with the antique décor, while the inside
would be modernized with the latest crime-fighting
equipment. The parking lot and day-to-day entrance
was placed at the rear. At the front of the building, just
above the entrance, hung a huge sign with only the ini-
tials "OPD".

The MCU detective received a suite on the second
floor, which contained an office and a situational dis-
cussion area. The SDA was outfitted with large white
boards for discussing crimes, two large flat-screen
televisions, large conference table, and a computer
command center with access to all police networks
throughout Virginia.

The back parking lot entrance led directly into the
main lounge of the OPD. Just outside the lounge to the
right were the stairs to the upper two floors. Lieutenant Dan Miller was still sitting in the lounge at a table
next to the coffee machines. He was drinking a cup of
java and listening to the early morning news report
that was playing on the new wall-mounted forty-eight
inch LCD.

"The TV broke in your office?" asks Jack as he enters through the door.

"It's about time you get your ass to work! You look like shit! Didn't get enough sleep this morning? And no, smartass, my TV works fine, just came in here to get my coffee refilled," Dan says.

"And who do you think woke me up this Sunday morning!"

In a more serious tone, Dan asks, "Are you going to be OK today?"

"Yep, just another day in paradise!" exclaims Jack. He knows that he will be in the limelight now. Onancock hadn't seen a murder in more than seven years. He also knows that if the victim was from NYC, he will have to work with the big-city detectives again, something he does not look forward to. He had always thought that detectives in the big cities thought of themselves as elitist and the small-town detectives as bumpkins. That was one of the reasons he left the Washington, DC police force; another reason was the politics. Big departments were cut throat and nasty. Getting promoted or assigned good cases often depended on political alliances. You had to suck up to get ahead.

The phone rings as Jack enters his office. He races

to his desk to grab the receiver. "Jack, need you in my office now." He recognizes the voice of Captain McClellan. Jack's office is at the back of the building on the second floor of the OPD. The second floor also houses the interrogation rooms and a set of restrooms. Jack is glad that his office is segregated from the rest of the squad rooms, but when he is summoned to the captain's office, he has to traverse the entire first floor.

As Jack passes through the large squad room, patrolmen watch a news reporter on the wall-mounted television. The reporter, Mary Johnson, is a young blonde bombshell that Jack once dated. She still can make his body flush. Jack had heard that she married the new pitcher for the Norfolk Tides, a baseball farm team for the Baltimore Orioles.

Mary reports from the beach with the Bay as a backdrop.

"This morning, according to the OPD spokesperson, a young woman was found murdered on our beach. Her identity is pending next-of-kin notification. The OPD has stated that this is an isolated incident and that our visitors and locals should not be afraid to enjoy the beaches. We have also been told that Detective Jack Sinclair will be leading the investigation. We will provide our viewers with more information as we get it. Back to you guys in the studio."

One of the patrolmen turns and sees Jack standing in the middle of the room. He stands, hands outstretched, and bows toward Jack. "Looks like you are going to be a television star now."

"Just what I fuckin' need!" exclaims Jack. He turns and sees Captain McClellan standing his doorway.

Jack enters Captain McClellan's office and is told to shut the door.

"What's up captain?"

"This is the first murder investigation that we have had since you've joined our force. What's your plan?"

"Captain, I haven't had the time to formulate a plan yet. The crime scene unit should be back by now. The M.E. will have a preliminary finding by this afternoon. I could prod Randy a little."

"Jack, this is going to be a helluva media frenzy from as far south as Virginia Beach all the way north to Baltimore. If you need anything let me know ASAP. OK?"

Jack figures he best get started so he heads to the morgue to see Randy. Medical examiners can be crucial to solving a case and Jack feels fortunate to have a reliable ally in Randy.

As Jack enters the morgue, he is struck by a familiar odor not encountered since his days with the DC police department. Randy sees Jack and points to the gloves, mask and Vicks jar just inside the doorway. Placing Vicks under your nose helps with diluting the decaying odor.

"I have just started with the autopsy. I don't have anything yet. You do have your preliminary crime scene report, don't you?" asks Randy.

Jack stands and watches Randy work for a time before responding.

"Not yet, the CSU team hasn't finished yet. Was there any evidence of a sexual attack?" asks Jack.

"No. It looks like the killer just wanted her dead. Her attire was untouched and no prints were left on the body or anything around it. The crime scene unit didn't find any shell casings at the scene. It looks like she was a target, Jack."

On his trek back to his office Jack mulls requesting assistance from New York. He knows it will be a pain in the ass; big city cops will want to brush him aside and, at the very least, be condescending. He worries about jurisdiction issues, remembering a case years ago he worked with the Maryland State Patrol. Even though the murder happened in DC, the Maryland cops wanted to take the lead on nearly every aspect of the investigation and use their own people.

"I hate that bullshit. I hate the politics," Jack grumbles.

Then, with a smile, he thinks: Captain McClellan wants to help! OK, I'll let him deal with that crap.

5

Jack sits at his desk, watching his laptop boot up.
The OPD had replaced the old desktop computers with
newer, quicker laptops with aircards to allow investigators flexibility while in the field. Jack considers himself
an old school detective—notepad and pen are all the
equipment he needs. Lightweight and quick! He takes
his laptop with him to crime scenes, but rarely uses it.

After taking a sip of his coffee, he searches Google
for as much information as he can find on the victim,
Janet Hastings. He's astonished by the amount of information that turns up.

"Janet Hastings graduated at the top of her class
at Columbia Law School. She passed the New York Bar
exam on her first try. After a few months as a public

defender, she decided that it was time to spread her wings in private practice, joining the firm Miles and Stratton Law Office. Janet soon started making a name for herself as an advocate of the criminally rich. If you had money and were in trouble, she was there to help. Her clientele became the "Who's Who of New York", as well as the international criminal world. Members of the infamous "Five Families" kept her on retainer. She received acquittals against three drug lords accused of cocaine distribution by showing that key witnesses against her clients were paid informants with criminal records. In another high profile court victory, she persuaded a judge to dismiss charges of embezzlement against a businessman because prosecutors improperly seized accounting records from the man's investment firm."

A newspaper reporter writing about Hastings described her as "notorious as a ruthless attorney, both inside and outside the court room, but also passionate about protecting the rights of her clients."

A prestigious business magazine featured Hastings on its cover. She stood with arms crossed, hair draped over her shoulders, a sly smile, and dressed in a Navy blue business suit with a collar open enough to show just a hint of cleavage. The headline read, "Not

Just a Pretty Face." The story told of Hastings's quick rise and how she was the envy of this youngest generation of lawyers. Miles and Stratton would take picks of the litter from New England and New York law schools. Typically, a job prospect would have to finish in the top one percent of the class and be invited to apply by a senior partner. Smart young prosecutors with the right pedigree were also recruited by the firm.

Hastings had the education, but she also had flair. She knew how to evoke admiration and attention without being overt. She instantly caught the eyes of many older males in the firm and the envy of others her age who were writing legal briefs, researching case law, reviewing contracts, and waiting for their big break. She sought out Miles and Stratton, knowing they couldn't refuse.

Within a year with the firm, Hastings made partner. She had leapfrogged over a generation of lawyers with seniority. The promotion shocked everyone inside the law firm except for the two co-founders who made the decisions. Their reason was strictly business. In an e-mail to the one-hundred-member firm, Mr. Miles and Mr. Stratton said simply that Ms. Hastings had shown exemplary skills as a trial lawyer and, as a result, landed the firm its biggest client ever.

That client, Tyrone Perkins, is a well-known crime boss posing as an entrepreneur. Federal and local law enforcers had tried building cases against him for more than a decade. They relied on paid informants or confessions from criminals looking to cut a deal to keep themselves out of jail; but Perkins was too shrewd to leave a paper trail or be recorded. Prosecutors were, however, unrelenting. Perkins knew he was prey and wanted protection, both for himself and his businesses.

Jack types "Tyrone Perkins" into his search engine, which delivers a string of news stories: "Tyrone Perkins is known throughout the state of New York, as well as throughout the international world, for being involved in drugs, gambling, prostitution, and anything that would be considered illegal," one newspaper article reported. " He covers his illegal wrongdoings with legitimate businesses throughout the world." A news blogger said, "The annual estimated net worth of his businesses range well over five hundred billion dollars. One could only speculate his own net worth."

He was not only an interesting figure in the United States, but he had become a person of interest to Interpol as well. Perkins had never been prosecuted within the United States for any drug, gambling, or any other criminal business dealings, but Interpol had been investigating him for his alleged criminal activity all throughout Europe.

In the so called "drug lord world," he is the only one considered "untouchable." None of the criminal activities could ever be traced back to him. He appears as a bona fide businessman.

Jack knows the Perkins connection will require that he contact the NYPD and, possibly, the feds. He also needs to consult with one other person. Jack picks up his phone and dials a four-digit extension.

"Captain, could you come to my office?"

"Jack, what's up? Why can't you come down here?"

"I have something that needs to be discussed privately and I prefer not to discuss it in your office! You will understand when you get here," Jack says. Captain McClellan's office is on the first floor just outside the main squad room. Even though his office has a door, the walls are built with glass upper panels, so that he can see into the squad room. The squad members can sometimes hear what is being said in his office, especially when voices are raised.

Within a couple of minutes, Captain McClellan enters Jack's office. Jack points to a chair next to him. Captain McClellan sits next to Jack and starts viewing the articles that Jack had found on the victim, her law firm, and the connections to Tyrone Perkins.

"What the hell have we gotten into this time? Are you speculating that this was a contract hit?" asks Captain McClellan.

"I wouldn't want to speculate, but with what Randy has already told me, this could definitely be a result of a contract hit. Maybe Janet and Tyrone had a breakup and he wanted to close any loose ends. I know I need to get the NYPD involved, but you know as well as I do, they will want to take over this case. What do you think the district attorney is going to say?" asks Jack.

"Jack, this is our town; even though a small town, it is still our town! The victim was murdered here! As far as I am concerned, we own this case and until I hear differently from the DA or the attorney general's office, we are in charge. You make your call and I will make my call to the DA's office." Captain McClellan rises and heads back to his office.

As Jack contemplates who to call, he remembers that Dan and his wife had visited New York City last year. Dan returned with a story of meeting a NYC detective who gave him a tour of a local precinct. Jack dials his old friend.

"Dan, I need your help." Jack catches Dan off guard and he knows it.

"OK, what's up, pal?" Dan responds.

"Do you remember telling me about your trip last year to New York?" Jack asks.

"Sure."

"Do you still have the contact information for the detective that you and your wife met there?"

Dan remembers his encounter with the NYC detective and that she had given him her business card. "Hold a sec, Jack." Dan pulls out his wallet and locates the card. "Yep, got it right here! Do you want me to bring it to you?"

"No, I'll come get it shortly," Jack says.

First, Jack wants to retrieve the evidence from CSU. He takes the stairwell and heads to the third floor.

The CSU lab takes up most of the third floor of the OPD. When Onancock became the site for the major crime unit, Captain McClellan requested the town council petition the state for a CSU lab that would mirror Norfolk's or Virginia Beach's. The lab could perform virtually all aspects of crime scene detection with the exception of DNA testing, which had to be performed in Richmond.

As he enters the lab, Jack sees Stacey Warwick, senior CSU technician, standing next to the waist-high sorting table that was built onto the rear wall of the lab.

Stacey is a tall redhead in her mid-thirties. She has the build of an Amazon warrior. Jack refers to her as the "goddess." Jack has fun watching all the single officers, and some older married guys perk up at crime scenes when Stacey shows up. Stacey loves the looks she gets from the new rookies. Jack reminds himself that Stacey is married to a six-foot-five former U.S. Marine, now a Virginia State Trooper.

Stacey is the newest addition to the OPD-CSU lab. She had been hired as the senior CSU tech, by Captain McClellan, to replace her retiring predecessor about two years ago.

"Afternoon Stacey, got anything ready for me yet?" exclaims Jack.

Stacey had been concentrating on tagging the evidence, so she doesn't hear Jack enter the lab. He startles her.

"Detective Sinclair, you could have made some noise as you entered. I almost dropped this evidence bottle."

"Sorry," Jack whispers. "I'll try to be louder next time." He smiles.

"Well, I'm finishing tagging the last of the evidence. I was going to call you. You must have been thinking of me. Were you, Jack?" she smirks and then winks. Stacey knows she's just flirting with Jack. He's a former Marine like her husband and Marines stick together.

Jack tells Stacey that she's been hanging around the M.E. too much because she is starting to act like him.

"Did you find anything interesting yet?" Jack asks without giving her the satisfaction of answering her last question.

"We found an impression of a person that appeared to be lying and squatting in the dune grasses approximately thirty to forty yards away from the victim. From the pictures we took, it appeared that the individual had been there for a few hours," Stacey says.

"So your assumption is that she was being watched. The watcher could either be the killer or a witness. Did you find anything that would show which one the watcher could be?"

"That is for you to find out. You are the detective, correct?" Stacey says. "What I do have are pictures of smudged footprints in the sand. What we don't have are footprints leading to the victim from the sand dune. We only have prints leading from the same direction you and everyone else took this morning. I am guessing that your stalker may have gone to the road and approached the victim from that same angle, that's if the stalker is the killer."

"We took plenty of pictures from inside the beach house that she had rented," Stacey continues. "Everything in the house was neat, clean and well organized. You wouldn't even have known she stayed there, if it wasn't for the neighbors. Not much to tell from the house since the murder took place on the beach. The pictures are in the evidence box."

While they talk, Stacey completes the tagging process and loads the evidence into an evidence box that reminds Jack of the paper-ream boxes that he had used to pack his desk when he left DC. Now it's his turn to review the evidence.

"I have to go see Lieutenant Miller for a minute. I will pick up the box on my way back. Is that OK with you?" asks Jack.

"Sure, I have to finish the written report anyway," Stacey says.

Jack leaves the lab and heads for his pal's office. Dan and Jack are close friends. They grew up in Onancock and even went to the same college together, both on football scholarships—Jack, a tight end and Dan, a defensive tackle. After college, Jack rejected an offer to join the Washington Redskins and joined the Marines instead. Desert Storm was in full swing and he felt it was his duty to serve his country first and foremost. Dan broke his shoulder during the playoff game of their senior year. He opted for the OPD. They stayed in touch through the years and when Jack left the Marines and joined the Washington, DC police force, Dan was elated. When Dan heard that a MCU detective position was coming available in Onancock, he immediately called Jack. Jack wanted so desperately to leave DC that he jumped at the position. Dan was delighted that Jack accepted the position, but was also worried that the small town atmosphere would be too mundane for him.

Dan looks up from his laptop and sees Jack crossing the squad room toward him. He had not told Jack that the business card that he had received while in New York belonged to a female detective. She is young, beautiful, and brash, just Jack's type. This could be fun to watch, Dan thinks to himself.

6

Detective Maggie Williams is nearing her seventh year as a NYPD major crime unit detective. Today she plans to finally break away from the bustle of the city for a well-deserved vacation. Co-workers have never seen Maggie take a vacation. She has always told colleagues that her vacations are the "down time" between cases.

She had kept her plans for a real vacation quiet. She had just finished her last case and had no other cases pending. Maggie isn't much of a clock watcher, but today she can't wait for the noon hour. She's excited!

As she sits at her desk, she lets her mind drift

back to her first few years on the police force. During her first year she had been decorated with the highest award given to a NYPD officer. She had stopped by Macy's Department Store on W 34th Street during her lunch hour for a birthday present for one of her brothers. When she entered Macy's she turned off her radio and did not hear the call for help from her fellow patrolmen. As she exited Macy's, she heard gunshots and hurried toward the sound. When she approached the corner of W 34th Street and 6th Avenue, she stumbled onto the scene of a shootout between two NYPD officers and two bank robbers outside the Chase Manhattan Bank. This corner was part of her beat assignment.

Until that moment she had been thinking about quitting and going back to school to become a lawyer, to fulfill her mother's wishes. Her dad was a cop which was, in part, why she became one. Police work was now part of her DNA. The urge to serve and protect had resurged. On the day of the shootout, she proved her grit.

Two patrolmen were pinned down when Maggie arrived. Both stayed crouched behind the squad car. Two robbers, both with handguns, fired 9mm bullets into the squad car. Several pedestrians scattered and screamed. The officers were poised to return fire but feared that someone innocent could be hit.

Maggie quickly grasped the situation. She was in uniform and didn't want to be noticed by the thieves. She watched the robbers fire another volley and then flee down the sidewalk. They were coming in Maggie's direction.

Maggie stepped inside a recessed entrance to a coffee store. She signaled for those inside to kneel. As the armed men dashed by, Maggie held her breath, counted to three and jumped onto the sidewalk from behind them. When they were about ten yards past she shouted, "Police officer! Stop and drop your weapons!"

The men looked over their shoulders. One swung around with his revolver. Maggie, crouching on one knee, fired first. The second thief spun, saw that the young officer had a bead on him, and surrendered. Maggie started trembling and her throat went dry as she continued to aim at the thief. Seconds later, the two patrolmen she assisted seized the men and cuffed them. The wounded thief would survive the shot to his upper right chest.

The crime scene was quickly flooded with other cops and an ambulance. Maggie credited the two patrolmen for their heroism. They handled the situation perfectly, she told investigators. It was Maggie's reputation that would flourish. She was presented the

NYPD Medal of Honor, the highest medal presented to a police officer.

Within the next few years Maggie became regarded as fearless but level-headed. She was one of the "good ones," someone with potential, someone respected by others. That wasn't an easy accolade to earn, especially for a woman. Men still run most cop shops and it's hard breaking into the club. Maggie was encouraged to apply for the major crime team. She had completed a MCU test case with flying colors.

Captain Reynolds, head of the major crime scene unit, had been watching the decorated detective in the Manhattan district. He was known for choosing only the best for his MCU team and thought it would be good to diversify his ranks. He sent over a request to her captain that he was going to offer her the team position. Being advised of the request, Maggie was elated. Her dream since she had been promoted to detective was to be chosen for a MCU team. That had been seven years ago. Seven years without a single vacation. Now it was time and she was definitely ready for a well-deserved vacation.

A ringing phone disrupts her daydreaming. Noon has arrived—time to leave. Rumor has spread that Maggie is actually taking a vacation. Her unit colleagues stand and applaud as she makes an embarrassing exit.

"Go back to work! For Christ's sake, it is only a vacation!" she shouts. They stay standing and watch. "Is it really happening?" one teammate whispers to another. Maggie looks toward her partner, Barry Carter, who has looked in her direction. The ringing came from his phone.

"Major crime unit!" Barry announces with the receiver in his ear.

Maggie's curiosity gets the best of her, and she stops her approach to the door. She wants to hear.

"This is Detective Jack Sinclair from the major crime unit in Onancock, Virginia. I would like to speak with Detective Maggie Williams. This is very important." Without even a "Please hold," Jack is immediately placed on hold and soft classical music begins playing in his ear.

Jack waits, thinking, Just who is Maggie Williams? Jack tries to picture her. Dan has not told him much about the NYPD detective. Is she old or young, tall or short, large or small? He listens to the music and lets his mind drift. He even begins to fantasize about her.

Barry turns and says, "Maggie, you have a call

from a detective in Virginia."

Maggie laughs, "Yeah, right. You take it."

"No really, it's a Detective Jack Sinclair from Onancock, Virginia and he asked for you directly."

The squad room roars with laughter. What did Barry say? "On a cock?" Maggie slowly turns from the door and shoots everyone a mean stare. The room quiets as she returns to her desk.

Irritated that Barry didn't take the call, Maggie jerks the receiver from his hand and says, "This had better not be a fuckin' joke, Detective Sinclair from 'On a cock, Virginia'!"

The greeting startles Jack, but he proceeds anyway. "Detective Williams, this is Detective Jack Sinclair from the Own-an-cock Police Department on the Eastern Shore of Virginia." He pronounces the city's name slowly for her benefit. He continues, "I was given your number from Lieutenant Dan Miller, who you met last year when he and his wife were visiting the city." Maggie is quiet for a few seconds, apparently trying to recall the visit. She finally remembers the meeting and she lets out a small chuckle. Barry watches Maggie and is surprised by her chuckle.

"Why, of course, Detective Sinclair, I remember now. How can I help a fellow detective from Virginia?"

She asks as Barry grimaces.

"We have a situation here in Onancock that I feel will require help from you or your department." Jack describes the preliminary findings as Maggie listens intently. The entire squad room stays quiet as team members wait for the end result of the call. Maggie's been silent too long; some are already betting the vacation is off.

"I haven't determined much about the victim, other than what I have read on the Internet; and what I have read is mighty interesting. I am only in the preliminary stage, but since she is from your city, I thought I'd give you a call for some background info. We have identified the victim as attorney Janet Hastings. Her major client is Tyrone Perkins, a very important person of interest. Do you happen to know how to contact him? I would definitely like to interview him in regards to this case," Jack says.

Maggie sits slowly in a desk chair. Cases that cross state lines always intrigue her. She knows the name Tyrone Perkins; she's known it since joining the MCU.

Janet is well known throughout the ranks of the NYPD, too. Maggie can tell from Jack's description of the crime scene, his nonchalant way of stating the information, that he doesn't fully comprehend the impact or significance of the situation that has dropped into his lap.

"Detective Sinclair, I need to call you back. Give me a number where I can reach you. It will be just a few minutes." Jack is stunned at the abruptness but he gives Maggie his phone number. What did he do to deserve that?

The entire squad room bursts into laughter as Maggie jumps from her chair and heads toward Captain Reynolds's office. "What a fuckin' way to start a vacation!" mutters Maggie.

7

On the drive back to the city, he keeps checking his e-mails on his new iPhone, hoping to see if anything is being posted about his kill. He has also been listening to the radio to see if anything was being reported about the situation in Onancock. He does not think that the radio stations throughout Maryland and Delaware would report a crime that happened in Virginia, but he hopes to hear something when entering New York.

With the new laws that are being discussed throughout the states on the Eastern seaboard about the dangers of texting and driving, he is being very cautious when checking e-mails. The last thing he needs today is to be pulled over for irresponsible driving. While checking his e-mail, he comes across one that appears to have been sent to an entire distribution group. The e-mail mentions an upcoming meeting between Henry Miles and an agent from Interpol, concerning Janet and her clients. His car swerves, so he pulls over to finish reading.

"Dammit!" he says. "What the hell does Henry think he is doing? Is he fuckin' crazy?" He finally realizes that he is actually yelling at his iPhone. His timeline for his next task has just been escalated. He needs to get to New York as soon as possible. He can't believe this is happening now! He's anal about keeping a tight schedule.

"Things will work out! Things will work out!" he repeats aloud.

8

During his Internet search, Jack ran across another article concerning another partner of the firm, Henry Miles. He had not mentioned this to Detective Williams because he wanted to investigate the partner on his own. Jack located the phone number for Miles and Stratton Law Office and called the number. A receptionist transferred him to Mr. Miles' secretary. Now for the second time today he is put on hold and listening to classical music.

Henry W. Miles, co-owner and senior partner of the law firm, had become curious of the billing transactions between Janet and client Tyrone Perkins. Payments had become irregular.

Henry was reviewing billing information that he had obtained on Janet and her clients when his secretary buzzed him over the telephone's intercom.

"Mr. Miles, you have a call on line one from a Mr. Samuel Anderson from the Interpol office here in Manhattan."

"Thanks, Martha," Henry says. "Also, please hold all my calls. I don't want to be disturbed."

As soon as the secretary releases the intercom, her phone rings again. The caller ID shows it's from the front desk receptionist. She presses the button for the second line and is greeted by the receptionist stating that a Detective Sinclair is calling for Mr. Miles.

Mr. Miles' secretary is smug. "Detective Sinclair, Mr. Miles is currently in a meeting and has asked not to be disturbed. Is there something that I can help you with?"

"No thanks, but could you tell Mr. Miles that I am from Virginia and that this call is in reference to Janet Hastings. I need to talk with him as soon as he can return my call." Jack gives the receptionist his contact information.

Henry presses the line one button on his phone. "Mr. Anderson, this is Henry Miles. What can I do for you today?" Henry does not want it known that he is investigating one of the firm's partners and clients, at least not yet.

"Mr. Miles, we have been provided information that your law firm now handles all of the business transactions and accounts for a Mr. Tyrone Perkins and his conglomerate. I would like to make an appointment with you and the attorney handling Mr. Perkins's accounts. Do you have availability today or tomorrow?"

Henry Miles is surprised to hear that an agent from Interpol is calling him. His own investigation had just uncovered Interpol's interest in regards to Janet and Tyrone. Is this a coincidence that he and Interpol are investigating the same thing?

"Mr. Anderson, the attorney handling Mr. Perkins is currently out of the office on vacation. I wouldn't mind meeting with you today. We can also meet again once she returns from her vacation, if the need arises."

Samuel thinks this request is odd, speculating that Henry Miles may know more than he lets on. Henry's statement "if the need arises" draws his interest, so why not meet with him alone. "Mr. Miles, what time did you have in mind?"

"How soon can you be in my office?" Henry asks.

"Give me an hour," Mr. Anderson says.

"OK, see you then."

Henry knows that "attorney-client confidentiality" could be used as a shield by lawyers not to discuss the affairs of their clients. But if there are criminal issues being hidden, he is obligated to investigate. Henry Miles does not want his firm to suffer from a misrepresentation or malpractice.

Henry pages his secretary. "I need you to cancel all of my appointments today except for Mr. Anderson. I do not want to be disturbed the rest of the day."

"Mr. Miles, while you were on the phone, a Detective Sinclair from Virginia called. He wants to speak with you about Janet."

"Did he say why he wanted to talk about Janet?" Henry asks.

"No sir, but he did leave his contact information."

"OK, I will get it from you later. If it was an emergency, he would have said so. I will call him either after my meeting with Mr. Anderson or tomorrow morning. Mr. Anderson will be here in about an hour." Henry hangs up the phone.

Detective Sinclair will have to wait his turn, Henry thinks as he returns to his reading.

An hour later, Henry's intercom rings.

"Mr. Miles, Mr. Anderson is here now."

"OK, Martha, show him in."

Samuel Anderson enters Miles's office with the flair of an Englishman. Henry walks around his desk and extends his hand. After the cordial introductions, Henry points to the conference table where he has placed the information of his investigation. For the next couple of hours, Henry and Samuel share their information. Henry notices that it is close to five. His driver will be waiting on him. Henry Miles is known for his compulsions.

Samuel leaves Henry's office with a sense of failure. Nothing Henry shared will help him with his investigation. "This was a waste of time," he mutters as he leaves the office.

9

"What the hell is wrong with the people in New York?" Jack mutters to himself. "Do they think they can just ignore me, just because I am from a small town in Virginia?" As Jack wallows, his phone rings.

"Jack, I want to first apologize for ending our earlier call abruptly," the voice says. "It's Maggie."

"That's OK. Was it something that I said?" Jack grimaces, thinking maybe he shouldn't have said that.

"No, but are you in a private area where you can talk?" she asks.

"Yes, I am in my office, but I'm starting to feel that I will need to contact my captain as well."

Maggie scowls. How does a detective in a small town in Virginia rate a private office and here in New York, you had to be a high-ranking police officer to get an office.

"Sure, if you want. How long do you need?" asks Maggie.

"Just a couple of minutes. Can you hold and I will call him now?"

Putting Maggie on hold evokes a smile from Jack.

"Captain, I need you to come to my office. I have the detective from New York on hold and she has some news that she would like to share with us. I think you need to be up here to hear it as well, just in case politics becomes an issue."

This is the second time Captain McClellan has been summoned by Jack, a subordinate. "What in the hell ever happened to police protocol?" he mumbles. Within two minutes, Captain McClellan walks into Jack's office. "Jack, I am your captain, you can't keep requesting me to your office. It should be the other way around." He was huffing and puffing like he just ran a marathon. "Should have taken the elevator. Those friggin' steps are going to kill me!" he says.

Jack knows the captain is kidding, because in the years that he has been part of the OPD, he has never been to Jack's office.

Captain McClellan runs the Onancock Police Department. He's within six months of retiring after thirty years. He had been the chief of police in a small city in West Virginia, but moved to Onancock to become the captain for the OPD and to make his plans for retirement. He now looks forward to the daily fishing on the Chesapeake Bay.

Jack motions to the empty chair in his office. Captain McClellan pulls the chair next to Jack's desk. Jack presses the blinking button on his phone and states, "Maggie, my captain is here now." He introduces Captain McClellan.

10

The killer knows that Henry leaves the office at five o'clock. He will have his driver take him to the condominium tower which houses Henry's penthouse. He will probably be sitting at his dining room table eating his evening meal. Henry is so predictable. He has not wavered from his routine for ten years. Some would say that they could set their clocks by his routines.

Henry's penthouse overlooks Manhattan. The walls are adorned with fabulous paintings that he has been collecting from around the world. Some of the works, like a Picasso pencil sketch and a 1917 Matisse oil painting, were handed down from his father and grandfather. Henry has never married and his only child is his collection. He spent tens of thousands of dollars collecting his favorite artists and most cherished works of Vincent Van Gogh, Edouard Manet, and Alfred Sisley.

Henry would often spend evenings after dinner searching for upcoming private auctions for art collectors. But tonight he focuses on the implications of his meeting with the Interpol agent. As he thinks about next steps to take, he is startled by an abrupt knocking at his door. How could someone get to his penthouse without his knowledge?

Henry peers through the peephole and recognizes the man on the other side.

"What are you doing here this evening?" Henry asks as he steps aside to allow his visitor to enter. He shuts the door and faces the visitor, who has not yet said one word.

"Why are you here?" Henry repeats. Those were the last words Henry spoke as he fell to the floor of his lavish Manhattan apartment.

As he stands over the bleeding body of Henry Miles, the killer wishes he could savor the moment, but he also knows that he cannot leave visual evidence of his visit. He had been pressured into completing this portion of his task earlier than planned. The killer is glad that Henry lived in the penthouse. No neighbors to worry about! He did not have time to plan this attack as he had done with Janet's murder. This is not his first visit to the apartment, so he knows how to enter and leave.

As he stands in Henry's home, the killer imagines that this should be the life he is living—a penthouse apartment overlooking Manhattan, the plush carpets and furniture, Nineteenth century paintings. Now he hopes that he can make that dream come true. He is one step closer.

His thoughts return to the bleeding body of Henry Miles. He knows that Henry had paid his dues and deserved all of the riches; but because of the injustice at the firm, Henry Miles deserved to die.

Henry knew that making Janet Hastings a partner would be controversial and provoke jealousy, but never to such a degree. With one last glance, the killer exits the beauty of the plush penthouse apartment the same way he had entered—silently and undetected.

11

The day began as Maggie had planned—no cases, watching the minutes tick by on the large clock by the exit door, and thinking about getting out of the city. No more. Her mind drifts back to work, realizing she is on the verge of a major case, speaking to a Virginia detective who may or may not know what the hell he is doing or what he stumbled into.

"Jack, you have already done some Internet research on Tyrone Perkins. So you should know that he's a cartel boss masquerading as a business mogul. He was educated in both the United States and England. He not only has business ties in the Americas, but also throughout Europe, Southeast Asia, and he is moving into Africa and China. He has several houses but mainly lives in Rio de Janeiro. He built his home in an area called Morro do Leme, Spanish for 'a beautiful hill at the end of the beach'. He's rarely seen outside of his Rio home, unless he needs to travel. He came to New York briefly to move all of his legal transactions to his attorney's new firm."

"So are you thinking that this Tyrone Perkins had a problem with his attorney and had her killed?" Captain McClellan interjects.

"I would not want to speculate who killed her, but some say she is the devil with a three-pronged trident."

"How can we help and what do you need from my detective?" asks Captain McClellan.

"Uh, Captain, I'm just beginning, there's more," Maggie responds.

Captain McClellan and Jack flash each other a whimsical glance. There's more?

"Henry Miles and Stanley Stratton were the two senior partners, as well as co-owners, of the firm. Janet convinced them to bring her into their firm as a partner after signing the Tyrone Perkins conglomerate contract. This signing would mean millions in billable hours for the firm, so it was an easy decision for the two senior partners."

Jack knows most of this from his own research. Captain McClellan seems overwhelmed. He knows that telling Jack to contact the detective from New York will turn his world upside down just as he is preparing for his retirement.

"So are you saying that our victim's death is linked to the law firm or Mr. Perkins, or both?" asks Captain McClellan.

Maggie continues: "Captain, we believe her death could possibly be linked directly to Tyrone, and it also may be linked to her firm. But the guy is an eel. He slivers out of everything. Witnesses disappear or change testimony, cases are suddenly thrown out, or evidence is lost. This guy has a network protecting him, including big-name lawyers. He's never been convicted or even jailed. Any investigation into his activities has either been squashed by his attorneys or by local authorities."

The captain sits back and groans. "There goes my retirement this year!"

"So, where are we on this thing?" Jack asks abruptly.

"I have asked my captain to allow me to travel to Virginia and work with Jack on this investigation,"

Maggie says. "Of course, that is if you agree, Captain McClellan. And, Jack, don't get pissed off with me. I'm not trying to take your case. If you want to interview suspects and witnesses, go ahead, but I want to be in the room too."

Captain McClellan sighs, nodding to Jack and then telling Maggie to come down for a meeting. "Let's be clear about one thing detective, you'll be assisting us. Got it?"

"OK, I'll see you gentlemen in about thirty-six hours. By the way Captain, the NYPD and the state of New York will foot the bill for the entire investigation." Captain McClellan knows the NYPD will try to commandeer the case.

"Just get down here ASAP," Captain McClellan tells Maggie. "We will have all of our evidence waiting for your review." He looks at Jack and says, "Jack, make sure we have everything from the M.E. and the crime scene techs ready for her arrival."

Maggie chimes in. "Oh, there is one last thing—this investigation has to be kept secret, and the communication that we have shared today should be kept confidential. We would like to keep everything quiet until we decide how to proceed. All medical examiner reports must not be released. Is that OK with you, Captain?"

Captain McClellan's tone hardens. "Look, we're not dumb asses. We don't release information to anybody when a case is being investigated. But we have a body of a young woman that was murdered on our beach. Our small community knows about it. The fucking TV stations have been knocking on doors and poking around. Newspapers from Washington, Baltimore, and Norfolk have been writing about this case. I can't do anything about that. You got it?"

"Captain McClellan, I know that you have an obligation to your community, but the least amount of information presented would be appreciated at this time. That's all I am asking. No media interview, OK? By the way, aren't there some outstanding murders in Virginia Beach involving young women? Can't you throw the press off by hinting that your case might be connected?"

Captain McClellan leans back into his chair. How do those shits in New York know about unsolved cases in Virginia Beach?

"Look, I'll handle the local media. And you try not to forget that this is a murder in our state."

Seconds after Captain Reynolds and Maggie Williams end the call, Jack erupts.

"What the fuck, captain! Are we going to let the

NYPD take over our investigation?"

"Jack, relax. We'll cooperate. They know a lot more about the victim and suspect then we do right now. Let me handle the politics. Anyway, Jack, the state AG's will ultimately make the call about who to charge and where. Until the suits decide, it's our case. The woman died in our jurisdiction."

Jack needs to get moving to stay ahead of the NYPD, so he heads for the door without acknowledging the captain.

"Jack, don't let those New York assholes show us up," the captain says.

12

Jack finds Randy sitting at his desk at the morgue. This is a rare sight. Every other time Jack has been here, the medical examiner has been leaning over one of the autopsy tables.

"How's it coming, Randy?" Jack asks.

Randy had just completed his penning of his preliminary autopsy report on the victim. He still hand writes his findings, and then transposes them to the computer. What would Maggie and her captain think? Jack wonders.

"What's up with you? Why do you keep busting my chops? Why the rush?" Randy demands.

"Randy, I'm sorry, but I have been ordered to keep this confidential," Jack says. "You will have to trust us on this one. We have a visitor coming from the NYPD to assist us in our investigation and I need something before she gets here."

"She? Hmm, no wonder you are in a hurry." Randy chuckles.

"Don't start. I have already heard it from Dan."

Randy smiles and then begins reading his preliminary finding. "Young woman approximately thirty-three years of age, well-manicured, and was in top physical shape. No signs of drug abuse, no signs of alcoholism, even though there was a wine glass at the scene. There were two gunshot wounds, one to the heart, no exit wound, and one to the head which travelled through the brain, again no exit wound. In my opinion, this shot was the second shot and was meant to make certain the victim died. The findings lead me to believe that this woman was a victim of..."

"A cold-blooded killing," finishes Jack.

"That too, Jack, but what I was going to say is that she was a victim of a planned and meticulous assassination. Fingerprint analysis and New York DMV information confirm the identity. Just as the neighbors had said, she is Janet Hastings."

Nothing new here, Jack thinks. "OK, thanks Randy. Could you forward me a soft copy as soon as possible?"

"No problem, it will be in your office within the next couple hours," Randy says. Randy knows that soft copy means a computer file, not a paper report. He is still getting used to this new computer world. "I still feel safer with paper," he mumbles.

Jack buys a Diet Coke from a vending machine in a hallway outside the morgue. Coke gives him a needed jolt, especially in the afternoons. As he takes a swig he wonders: Why would a cold-blooded killer enter into our small town just to kill an outsider? The killer had to know this person or had been contracted to kill her.

13

Maggie went through the same mental paces in New York. Sipping a Diet Pepsi, she too puzzles over the seeming randomness of the crime. Her killer had to know the victim was in Onancock. Who else would have known she was there? A big name attorney with ties to Tyrone Perkins. It had to be a hit.

This is no coincidence? she thinks. Maggie doesn't believe in fate, but to be called about a case that involved a person from her past—as a result of a short meeting, a year ago, with a police lieutenant and his wife, from a small town in Virginia. Weird!

This was the second time that Tyrone Perkins's

name has crossed her desk. The first time was when she had just been assigned to the major crime squad. Tyrone was a person of interest in a local murder investigation, which also included victims that were members of the "Five Families" in New York. Speculation was that he was eliminating his NY competition.

Since she was the new kid on the block, she was given the case file to review and investigate. To the astonishment of One Police Plaza, she was making greater headway than anticipated. Two weeks into the investigation, though, the file and all of her investigative notes were pulled from her.

Maggie was confounded. What had she done wrong? It was her first case with the MCU. All of the files and the notes she had acquired during the short investigation were being placed into boxes and sealed by her partner. She was called into her captain's office, a large room encircled by glass walls with ceiling to floor blinds. Maggie noticed that the blinds had been closed as she approached the office. When she entered, she was stunned to see the chief of detectives for all of the New York City boroughs sitting on a sofa.

Maggie remembers when the entire squad had pooled their money and bought the sofa. It replaced the shabby antique that had been in the captain's office since the early 1980s. Maggie had only seen the chief once before, early in her career, at her award ceremony. She had never seen him here, or even at the precinct where she had worked prior to joining the MCU team.

"Maggie, please take a seat," Captain Reynolds said.

She sat in one of the large cushion chairs situated across and facing the overstuffed sofa where the chief was sitting. Captain Reynolds joined the chief on the sofa and started.

"Maggie, we appreciate the diligence that you have shown these past two weeks with your current case. The pulling of the files has nothing to do with your ability as a detective."

The chief chimed in, "Detective Williams, your reputation is well known at One Police Plaza. You are one of our best detectives. The decision to stop this investigation has come from the state attorney general's office, with the approval of the governor. Tyrone Perkins will no longer be investigated by the NYPD at this time. You are not to proceed with any inquiries into any of his businesses. We apologize that this was handled this way, but we hope you understand the sensitivity of this request."

Maggie didn't get ahead by disobeying orders

from her superiors, and she wasn't going to start now. The name Tyrone Perkins really didn't mean anything to her at the time.

"Captain, Chief, I understand and I will consider this case closed."

As the chief rose from the sofa, he extended his hand to Maggie, thanked both of them and then walked out of Captain Reynolds's office.

That was five years ago. This time Tyrone's case file wasn't going to be pulled from her. This was going to be her case, even if she had to "sweet talk" it from the country cops of the Onancock Police Department.

Maggie had never traveled farther south than the shores of Atlantic City, New Jersey. Now she was heading to a backwater town called Onancock. Maggie opens her laptop and her web browser to Google and searches for this small town. Who would name their city Onancock? Where was this place? What did it have to offer? Where could she stay? Why did Janet go there? All of a sudden, her mind turns to her own vacation plans. If Janet went there for a get-away vacation, maybe she should stop her complaining and consider the trip a vacation too.

As Maggie reads articles on the Internet about Onancock, she finds one describing the OPD: "The

Onancock Police Department is one of the two major police departments on the Eastern Shore that has a major crime unit. The Eastern Shore is divided by two counties, Accomack County and Northampton County. The OPD is located in Accomack County, which is the northern county of the Eastern Shore. Governor Tim Kaine had determined that the Eastern Shore of Virginia needed crime scene detectives in that area. He created two major crime units on the Eastern Shore, one for the southern area and one for the northern area, with one detective assigned to each of the units."

She wonders what it would be like to be one of only two detectives for an area of seventy miles. Her team in Manhattan had twelve detectives for an area of only thirty-three square miles.

She wonders about what clothes to pack. She's going there for business, not pleasure, but if the situation arises, she might be convinced to enjoy the scenery and shops.

14

Maggie never liked reading maps and was happy to have a GPS in her 2009 Mercedes C300 for her trip to Virginia. She had bought the C300 new but hadn't driven it much. There wasn't much need to drive in the city since she lived so close to the precinct. The only time she drove it was when she visited her parents in White Plains. This trip to Virginia would be her longest, giving her time to bond with her Benz. She left the city by way of the Lincoln Tunnel and headed toward Secaucus, New Jersey, where she caught the New Jersey turnpike south toward Wilmington, Delaware. Once over the bridge she would drive east toward the ocean and then south on route 13 through Delaware, Maryland, and into Virginia.

As a police officer, she had a duty to stay within the speed limit, but as a Mercedes owner, she let the C300 roar on some of the more desolate stretches of highway. If pulled over by the backwater cops, she could always flash her badge or big smile.

The trees are full of leaves that blow in the May breezes. The wild flowers along the highway are in full bloom. They give the appearance of bouncing rainbows along the roads, beautiful colors, and wonderful smells. Just outside Wilmington, she sees in the median a large area of wild flowers displaying every color imaginable. She has to have a picture of this breathtaking view. No one back home would believe her. As she is taking pictures, she imagines she sees Dorothy running through the Field of Dreams, searching for the Wizard. She smiles and says, "It is definitely beautiful here."

She climbs back into her car and wonders, With all that has happened, will Jack Sinclair be my Wizard? She starts humming, "We're off to see the Wizard..."

15

Virginia's Eastern Shore narrows into a thin finger of land as it stretches south. To the east is the Atlantic Ocean with small tourist towns and farms. The west is flanked by the Chesapeake Bay and the tributaries feeding it. The Shore's roots run deep in modern America. The seafood-rich Bay attracted colonial era settlers who fished the waters and farmed lands along creeks. Many of their ancestors remain, apparent by a peculiar brogue that sounds almost like a New England accent.

Most of the Shore, even its tourist towns, remains rustic. Local land owners have largely opposed the grand-scale development encouraged north on Maryland's Eastern Shore or to the south across the Bay in the Virginia Beach-Norfolk area known as Hampton Roads. Villages like Onancock lack the amenities of more popular travel havens and offer, instead, a more laid-back, reclusive escape. That must have been what lured Janet Hastings here, Maggie thinks as she passes by old general stores and soybean fields.

She is tired and anxious to arrive after seven hours of driving. The GPS directs her to the Onancock cop shop but she can't figure out where to park. There has to be an employee parking lot, even in this small town. Do they walk to work?

She knows she is at the right building because of the large OPD sign above the door. The building does not look like a police department, but being from the city, some of their buildings didn't look like police stations either. She also notices that there were parking spots in front of every building adjacent to the precinct, but none here. She drives around back and finds a few parked squad cars and unmarked vehicles. Not many people around, she thinks.

Maggie enters through the front door of the precinct. The receptionist reminds her of an elderly librarian just waiting to shush her. "I am Detective Maggie

Williams from New York City and I am looking for Detective Jack Sinclair, please."

The face of the receptionist lights up like a child's on Christmas morning, "You are from New York City, the Big Apple! Do you know Donald Trump? I am a big fan of his television show, *Celebrity Apprentice*. Do you think you could get me an autographed picture of him?"

The receptionist obviously has never been to New York.

"Excuse me, but Detective Sinclair, please," Maggie repeats.

The receptionist mutters something inaudible. She picks up the phone to call Jack's office. After the receptionist dials, she points to a set of chairs to the right of the entrance. Maggie is told to have a seat as if she was being punished by a librarian.

Jack's been reviewing the evidence and photographs from the CSU team. The photographs had refreshed his memory of the beach scene as well as the beach house. He is taking notes when the receptionist calls.

"Detective Sinclair, you have a visitor from New York in the main lobby."

Jack thanks the receptionist. Knowing it's probably Maggie, he calls Dan, who already met her last year and would probably recognize her.

"Dan, I think Detective Williams is in the front lobby. Since you've already have met her, could you meet with her first? I'll be right down."

"No problem pal, but don't think I am now your man servant." Dan laughs and hangs up before Jack can respond. He heads for the lobby.

Detective Maggie Williams is in her early thirties, with long brunette hair and probably weighs about one-twenty soaking wet. She has the body of someone who spends lots of time in the gym. She's exactly how Dan remembered her.

In defiance of the "librarian," Maggie stands and views pictures along the side wall of the reception area. Several are prints of Eastern Shore landscapes or birds. Dan's voice startles her.

"Glad to meet you again, Detective Williams, I'm Lieutenant Dan Miller. I wasn't sure you would remember me when I had Jack call you."

Maggie is cordial and says, "I thought I would be meeting with Detective Sinclair."

"Oh, he is on the way, but I thought I would meet with you as well."

"I have to admit, I didn't remember the meeting

at first, when Jack mentioned your name; but after a few seconds, I remembered our first encounter. So, how are your wife and daughter? Nancy and Elizabeth, right?" Maggie asks.

"They are well, and thanks for asking. You ready to meet Jack?"

Dan was going to describe Jack to Maggie, but thought, what the hell, let him make the first impression himself. Just then, he hears the elevator door open and he turns to see Jack emerging.

Maggie is not what Jack Sinclair had pictured at all. Dan thinks Jack is going to hit the floor by the expression on his face. As Maggie walks toward Jack, her long, flowing brunette hair, and curvy physique mesmerize him. His hormones surge. How will he keep this professional? Can he?

Jack imagines stroking her long hair and feeling her small, but firm, warm body press against his. She could be the one to end his bachelorism. Jack shakes his head as if he's trying to make the thoughts flow out of his ears. Jack, you're a professional, he thinks. Snap out of your daydream. Get your shit together. This is another detective.

"Detective Jack Sinclair," Jack says as he extends his hand. "How was your trip? I see you found us alright. I hope that we have time to give you a tour of our lovely beach while you're here." Dan laughs to himself at Jack's babbling. The cool bachelor seems like a dork.

Maggie's thoughts also drift into the personal. Jack is a handsome man, she thinks, well-built, fit. He must spend lots of time in a gym, too. Nice dark brown eyes, nice hair, and a nice smile. She feels tiny goose bumps developing along her spine.

She stops herself and thinks, Come on Maggie, get a grip. You don't date your fellow cops. You are here for business, not pleasure!

Maggie sobers when Jack says, "Shall we go to my office now?"

Again, Maggie hears the comment "my office." She still can't believe that he, a small-town, backwater detective, has an office and she has to share a large room with another team. A sign on a door at the end of the long hallway reads: Major Crimes, Detective Jack Sinclair.

Jack escorts Maggie into a space the size of three of the interrogation rooms back at her own precinct. She notices the large antique knotty-pine conference table in the middle of the room. She notices the table's ocean theme with shells, sand, and miniature bay creatures covered with a macramé coating. There's a modern conference-style phone in the middle of the table.

 Jack's desk abuts one of the side walls with a window. An office and a window view, she thinks she could live with this comfort. She sees an empty evidence box along with the contents stacked in well-organized piles at one end of the table. She turns toward Jack's desk and sees him bending over a small file cabinet. Her mind races again—nice ass, she thinks. Jack turns with two plastic water bottles in his hand. She blushes! It isn't a file cabinet after all, but a small refrigerator. What else does this room have in it, a bed?

 Jack carries the two water bottles to the conference table and hands one to Maggie. He motions for her to sit and he stares at her for a couple of seconds before he begins. He notices that she is blushing, but ignores it.

 "Maggie, before we start, I would like to know why you are here exactly, and don't just say it's because I called you. What about this case intrigues you?"

 Maggie anticipated the question, but not so soon. "I know you thought I was going to come here into your town and take over your case. As much as I would like to do that, this is still a murder within your jurisdiction. Even though it may have ties to one in our jurisdiction, this one is yours. After we find the individual, or individuals, that killed your victim, we can let the DA's work out the politics. Now let me give you some background on Janet Hastings."

Maggie shares the files that she had brought on Janet Hastings. Maggie explains that Janet owned a penthouse condominium in Manhattan and that there were rumors that she also had homes in the Grand Cayman Islands, Bahamas, and Cozumel, Mexico. Even though she had an array of clients, her closest and most notorious one was Tyrone Perkins.

"What we have ascertained so far, is that Janet Hastings, unbeknownst to her, was being investigated by one of the partners at Miles and Stratton. Henry Miles, senior partner, began to have second thoughts about bringing Janet into the firm. He also received a call from Interpol. With that call, Henry found out that Interpol was also investigating Tyrone Perkins and had just added Janet to their investigation as well. Henry met with Interpol just two days ago."

Jack is astounded by this information. This case is big, really big!

Jack asks, "So, what do you want of us? We can investigate what we have here, which shouldn't take very long, but it appears that most of this investigation is going to reside in New York."

"That may be true, Jack, but let's see what you have here for now," Maggie says.

"Yep, I suppose we have a killer to catch," Jack quips, and with that comment they get down to business going through the evidence on the table.

16

It's close to eight by the time they finish reviewing the evidence collected from the Onancock crime scene and the files Maggie had brought. Maggie's stomach growls again. She hasn't eaten since around noon and still hasn't booked a room. She looks up from the evidence and says, "Where's your nearest Hilton, Jack? Any decent seafood restaurants in this town? I am tired and hungry now."

Maggie leans back in her chair to stretch her now aching back and closes her eyes. Her long brunette hair falls lightly across the back of the chair. Her well pronounced breasts extend skyward.

Jack glances away from the folder he was studying and looks toward Maggie. She opens her eyes and catches his stare. Now he is blushing. Jack's face turns red as he turns his gaze from her.

A man hasn't looked at me that way in a long time, Maggie thinks. She feels feminine and flirtatious again. I guess when men find out you're a cop, they look at you differently, she thinks.

"Maggie, there's no Hilton here, but we do have a Days Inn and a Holiday Inn. And of course, we have seafood, fresh stuff from the Bay.

"Why don't you leave your car here and I will take you to the hotel of your choosing and pick you up in the morning. We then can stop and have a nice Southern breakfast before we return to the station."

Jack explains that the Holiday Inn is located on the beach, near the crime scene. The Days Inn is closer to the precinct. Maggie opts for the Holiday Inn. She might get a chance to go to the beach before she leaves Onancock. It would also allow her to see the Chesapeake Bay if she gets a room with a view. They restack the evidence and head for the stairs outside Jack's office.

As they walk out the back door of the OPD, Maggie looks over the parking lot at her Benz. "Jack, are you sure my car will be OK here?"

"Yep, no problem. Let's get your things and put them in my car."

Jack assists Maggie with her bags. "Which car is yours?" she asks.

He is quiet, but walks to his Jaguar parked a few spaces away. The surprises just keep coming, Maggie thinks. Jack places her bags into the back seat of the Jag and opens the door for her.

"You are such a Southern gentleman, Mr. Jack Sinclair," says Maggie, trying to mimic a Southern drawl.

Maggie and Jack head toward "All You Can Eat" seafood buffet, his favorite. Maggie has been to buffets in New York, but never to one with so much fresh seafood.

They sit in a rustic wooden booth. Maggie's plate is loaded with shrimp, oysters, and two fish fillets. A waitress brings them each a draft beer. Maggie has some appetite for such a slender person, Jack thinks.

Maggie quizzes Jack about his past throughout the meal. To Jack it almost feels like an interrogation. He tells about being raised locally, the Marines, being a cop in a big city. He wants to know more about her too, but she just keeps asking him more personal questions. Married? Kids? Parents alive? What do you do for fun? Do you work out? Sports?

Both avoid conversation about the case. There will be plenty of time for that. Tonight is about them.

Maggie makes two trips to the buffet and tells Jack it's the best seafood that she has had in years.

"I think it is second only to the Yankee Lobster Fish Market restaurant in Boston."

"Second only to Boston? Well, I guess, I'll take that as a compliment," Jack quips.

"Now I just need to get checked into the hotel. Where am I staying again?" Maggie asks.

Jack wants to say "my house," but instead pays the bill.

Maggie sits quietly absorbing the scenery of Onancock as Jack drives to the Holiday Inn. She sees a row of large beach houses with decks facing the beach. She is impressed by the affluence in such a small, seemingly backwater town. She starts to imagine what Janet must have felt her first day here. Maggie isn't much of a beach person, being raised in the concrete world of New York, but this breathtaking view makes her reconsider. Perhaps after this case, she will take that much-needed vacation at a beach.

Jack pulls up to the Holiday Inn. "Go ahead and

get checked into the hotel. I'll bring in your bags." As she starts to turn toward the door, he tells her that he will be back to get her early in the morning.

She smiles and stares into Jack's eyes for a few silent moments. "Thanks, Jack. I'll see you in the morning."

The parking lot and lobby are empty. Vacation season is still about a month away, so getting a room shouldn't be a problem.

The young man at the front desk looks as if he is still in high school; a young boyish look, but very polite. Maggie asks for a room and gives her name. "Ma'am, we have a room already reserved for you."

To Maggie's surprise Jack had reserved the room for a week. The young man assists her with her luggage. She wants to tip him but he says the gratuity has already been taken care of. She pulls the door closed, walks over to the window, and opens the heavy dark curtains.

"Oh my God!" exclaims Maggie. "What an amazing sight!" The Chesapeake Bay and the rolling waves meeting the beach sand fill the horizon. A full moon is bright enough to cast shadows. It would never be that bright in New York, she thinks. She stands and stares, rubbing her neck and rolling the stiffness from her shoulders.

The events of the day suddenly overcome Maggie. She feels exhausted. Time for a shower and bed. She thinks of Jack as the warm water runs down her back and legs. She keeps thinking of what it would be like to have Jack lather her body—her entire body.

Her body now dried, she dons her satin nightgown and walks toward the large window again. She takes in another view of the beauty of the moonlight bouncing on the Chesapeake Bay and pulls the curtains closed. She decides not to set the alarm; she'll awaken before Jack returns in the morning. She turns off the lamp on the oak side table and within minutes, she's asleep.

17

Maggie is roused by banging. Numbers on the digital clock on the nightstand blink because she hadn't set them. It's still dark. She rolls over and attempts to go back to sleep but hears the banging noise again. She groggily rolls out of bed and heads for the door.

Looking through the peephole, she sees Jack Sinclair standing in the hallway. What is he doing here? She then remembers that he said he would return to get her in the morning. Could it be morning already?

Maggie runs to open the curtains. The day welcomes her with the bright sunlight bouncing off the bay. She hadn't slept so soundly in months. It is a wonderful feeling.

She hears the knocking again. "Jack, I am up and I will meet you in the lobby in twenty minutes."

Sitting on a soft cushioned highback chair, Jack watches the local news program on a small flat-screen television mounted in the continental breakfast area. He hears the elevator door open and turns. Maggie strolls into the lobby and catches Jack's gaze. He's awestruck! She looks refreshed and beautiful. His gaze is focused on her during her entire walk from the elevator to the breakfast area.

As she reaches for a bagel, Jack tells Maggie not to get anything to eat yet, Dan is waiting for them.

"I have to eat something, Jack."

"Grab your coffee, or juice, and let's go. We're meeting Dan for breakfast." Dan and Jack often have breakfast together before starting their day. Within five minutes, they arrive at the local Waffle House. Inside, Dan sits in their usual booth.

Dan orders his usual—two eggs, hash browns, two slices of bacon, and grits. Jack follows suit except he substitutes the bacon for two slices of home-grown Virginia ham. Maggie orders a bagel with cream cheese and some fruit, just as she would have if she had been home. She has never heard of grits. Jack grins at Maggie and says, "I don't know how you plan to survive the day with just a bagel and fruit. We have a lot of work and it may be a long time before lunch."

As they sit eating their meals and drinking coffee, Dan and Maggie reminisce. Dan and his wife had gone to New York to see the *Lion King* musical on Broadway for their anniversary. They had left their daughter with his wife's mother for the weekend. Being an avid viewer of *Project Runway*, his wife wanted to view the Fashion District and Parsons School of Design. They had just left the Fashion District and were walking back to their hotel, through Times Square, when Dan saw a police precinct headquarters. He was curious about where "big city" detectives worked. As he and his wife entered the station they ran into Detective Maggie Williams, literally, almost knocking her to the floor. After some embarrassing apologies and cordial introductions, Maggie gave Dan and his wife a quick tour and introduced them to other detectives.

"Yep, some story, huh!" says Dan laughing. "A New York cop showing us such Southern hospitality."

The air smells sweet to Maggie as she and Jack head toward the Onancock precinct office. Just a few cars on the road, no sirens or honking horns. Newly blossoming flowers in pots dangle from the street lamps, and residents walk their dogs. How quaint, how quiet. She could get used to this!

Jack and Maggie head to the morgue first to meet with Randy, the medical examiner. The lights in the morgue are still off and no Randy in sight. Maggie, trying to peer into the lab, says, "I guess your M.E. works banker's hours in this small town."

Behind her a voice bellows, "I may have banker's hours, but I am here now. Who is the beauty with the attitude?" Randy asks Jack. "Life is too short to always be in a hurry, honey. At my age, banker's hours are a good thing."

Maggie is embarrassed, and Jack can tell.

Randy has a McDonald's bag in one hand and a half-eaten hash brown in the other. He puts the hash brown into the bag and reaches into his pocket to retrieve his office keys. "So again, Jack, who is the beauty with the attitude?"

"I am Detective Maggie Williams from New York, and I am so sorry for my comment. I didn't mean to insult you."

"It's OK, Detective Maggie Williams from New York. I am only messing with you! Apparently Jack hasn't told you about me. Shame on you, Jack! You left the lamb for the lion. You owe me one now!"

Randy is in his early sixties, with graying hair. Despite the McDonald's breakfast, he looks fit, trim, and tan. Glasses hang from his neck.

"I guess you both are here to get my autopsy results."

He begins with the same information that he gave Jack earlier. "The victim was well, fit, and young. She had been sleeping on the beach, in a wooden sun chair. She apparently was unaware of her killer's arrival. My assumption is that she was awoken just prior to being shot. She died instantaneously as the result of two gunshot wounds, either of which could have been the kill shot. In my opinion, the second shot was delivered to the head to ensure instant death. According to the ballistics report, the killer used a left-handed twist 9mm with a silencer."

Maggie stops Randy. "Are you sure it was about the twist of the 9mm?"

"Yes, I'm sure. I sent the bullets to the crime lab in Richmond and received an e-mail with their findings late last night. Why, is that significant?"

Maggie turns to Jack. "Remember me telling you about my first case as a MCU detective that was pulled from me by my captain and the chief. The perpetrator in that case also used a left-hand twist 9mm with a silencer. I need to make a phone call when we are done here."

18

Back at Jack's office, Maggie uses the conference phone on the table to call her partner, Detective Barry Carter.

"Hey Barry, how are things back home?"

"Just fine. Enjoying your vacation? Detective Sinclair, have you seen her in a bikini yet?"

"Knock it off, Barry. You've never seen me in a bikini."

"Listen, Maggie, I have some other news for you. Henry Miles was investigating Janet and her dealings with her clients. According to his secretary, he had a meeting with an Interpol agent just after you left. Shortly after that meeting he was killed in his Manhattan pent-house apartment by a gunshot to the heart and one to the head. His housekeeper found him the next morning.

"There was no forced entry, so it looks like he let the killer in. Nothing shows up on surveillance cameras, either, which may mean the guy knew his way around the building."

"Did you say that Mr. Miles was killed the night Maggie left New York for here?" Jack asks.

"Yep, that's right."

"Well, I called him that same day to talk with him about the Internet research that I found on Janet. I was told by his secretary that he was in a meeting and would call me back."

"Barry, you need to get the captain on the line. I need to talk with him now. We have encountered a disturbing event that concerns him," Maggie interjects.

Within seconds, Captain Reynolds says, "OK, Maggie, I'm here. What's up?"

"Captain, do you remember the first case that I was given when I first joined the MCU? After a couple of months, you and the chief told me that the case was closed and I was not to investigate it any longer. Do you remember?"

"Maggie, I remember what we told you."

"When I was investigating the case, before it was pulled, it was a case of a murder victim with two gunshot wounds; one to the heart and the other to the head. The M.E. that performed that autopsy stated that the bullets were from a left-hand twist 9mm with a silencer. The same type of weapon was used on Janet Hastings here in Onancock. I am willing to bet our M.E. will pull the same bullets from Henry Miles."

"Captain, I need the original files that were taken from me. Captain, I want to reopen that case and combine it with these two," she continues.

There is a long silence. Jack remains quiet. This is an NYPD issue, not his.

Captain Reynolds tells Maggie he'll speak to the chief. The DA will also have to be consulted.

"No guarantees, Maggie, but I'll do what I can. Chill out until you hear from me. Got it?"

"Guys, I am sorry that you now are involved with my ghost," Maggie tells Jack and Barry. "These murders are connected; at least that's my hunch. I am also guessing that Tyrone Perkins is either involved with these cases or, worst-case scenario, he is being framed for these murders. I don't want to believe the latter, but it is a possibility."

In his mind, Jack hears the tiny voices say, "They are taking your case!"

19

Cool breezes and warm sun are typical for this time of the year in Rio de Janeiro. Tyrone Perkins sits on his veranda sipping a cool mango flavored ice tea, looking out over the shores toward the southern Atlantic Ocean. He loves the high mountains, the view, and mango juice fresh squeezed from fruit picked on his estate.

He'll move his family to the Northern Hemisphere in a few weeks once winter settles in. He likes the outdoors too much to be cooped up inside during the cold. Tyrone prefers his yacht. He routinely uses it to host parties and board meetings. Most of the time, anything other than a swimsuit is considered overdressed.

Tyrone keeps his business away from his family, never holding meetings in his home. His yacht has state-of-the-art technology that connects to land services when docked and to satellites when at sea. A good day for Tyrone is dealing with business in the morning and sport fishing in the afternoon.

Tyrone loves competition—two CEO's sparring over mergers and buyouts or an angler battling a big fish on the hook. The latter being his preferred competition. He has landed great white sharks off the coast of Australia and giant tuna off the coast of Virginia. His favorite quarry is mighty blue marlin. He had once struggled for over two hours before conquering a five-footer.

Today, business is top of mind. Janet Hastings had sent him paperwork that had arrived earlier in the week requiring his review and approval. Inside is a letter from her stating that the United States Internal Revenue Service is looking into TexArMana Fruits; located in Shreveport, Dallas, Houston, and Atlanta. She says that she is not worried about anything in particular, but wants Mr. Perkins to be aware of the inquiry and of the documents requested by the IRS. Tyrone called his board to join him in Rio for a meeting.

Manuel Gonzales, president of TexArMana Fruits, speaks nervously. "Sir, I am not aware of anything that the IRS is investigating at TexArMana Fruits. Our CFO has reported nothing abnormal in our businesses. In fact, you should be receiving the latest set of spreadsheets for your review as we speak. I do not know where she got this information."

Matthew Brenner, president of New England Foods, interjects. "Mr. Perkins, there is something else you should know about what is going on in New York. I apologize for dropping this on you, but this could be an issue."

"What have you heard?" asks Tyrone.

"Henry Miles, Janet's partner, had a meeting with Interpol about their interest in you and Janet."

Tyrone knows about Interpol's investigation. The agency has been hounding him for two decades. The Henry Miles news is curious. Tyrone wonders if Janet had slipped up by sharing information to her partners at the law firm.

"Anything else that I should know?" Tyrone asks.

"Janet appears to have left New York two days before Henry Miles met with Interpol," Matthew continues.

Where is Janet? he thinks. He hadn't heard from

her. He had been trying to reach her since receiving the folder. This was not like her, she was usually very prompt in returning his calls. He did remember that she had planned a vacation. Maybe she hadn't returned yet.

Tyrone's cell phone rings just at that moment. It's a line only used by the personal assistant to contact him.

"Oh my, oh shit! When did it happen? Who knows?" Tyrone's voice is grim and shaky.

News of Henry Miles's death startles both Tyrone and his board. The implications are not yet clear, but no good will come of this. It will give Interpol another reason to dog Tyrone and his businesses.

The news Tyrone has just received from his assistant is twice as bad.

"Get the plane ready. Wheels up in thirty," he tells his assistant.

He stands. "Sorry gentlemen, our situation just got worse. Henry Miles is also dead. Be safe on your flights back to your homes. We'll talk later."

20

Jack can't shake the image of Maggie in a bikini. He reminds himself to be a professional, and not to be obnoxious. She has definitely warmed up to him, but is she interested, really interested? How can he find out?

"Maggie, quit what you're doing and let's go to lunch, my treat!"

"Where to?"

''Your choice," he says.

They decide to walk the "strip" in front of the precinct. Maggie soon sees Louie's Subs.

"Jack, here!"

He's surprised. She wants a sandwich?

"We can do better than this," he says.

Maggie orders a Philly Cheese Steak and wolfs it down like she's in a hurry. There was nothing romantic about this meal.

"Jack, when we leave, we have to go by that souvenir shop before we head back to the precinct." Maggie wants to get something just to prove she was actually in Virginia.

"What is it like to be a MCU detective in New York?" Jack asks. Maggie talks about her caseload, never having time to vacation, about the murders and assaults, which are routine in New York. She tells some about her dad being a cop, her brothers, how her mom wanted her to be a lawyer, and about how tough police work can be on a family. That's one reason why she has never married. She asks Jack about his career and whether he misses big city police work.

"After I left the Marines I went to DC for a while and then came home. I missed small-town living. You may not know this—I am one of only two MCU detectives on the entire Virginia Eastern Shore. I take care of all the major crimes from the middle-Shore north to the Maryland border.

"We get a lot of drug cases here and DUIs, especially in the summer with the migrant population. Lots of workers from Mexico and Honduras come here to pick crops. They mostly keep to themselves in farm housing, but sometimes they get boozed up.

"We have a lot of dope smokers, too. Commercial fishermen are the worse. They buy the stuff from locals growing it on their farms and get stone when they're pulling crab pots or netting bait fish. The Shore is also a pipeline for drug runners between your wonderful city and Virginia Beach.

"We have a problem with cars being illegally registered. Lots of times we'll find an old car with fake plates abandoned in ditches or crunched up against a road sign. It's pretty bland stuff compared to New York, I'm sure."

As they leave the sub shop, Maggie spots Sally's Ice Cream Parlor on the next block.

"Jack, do you know when the last time was I saw an ice cream parlor that looked like this one?"

Jack walks in silence just admiring her new girlish attitude. It is nice and different from what he had seen earlier. She's actually enjoying herself.

"When I was a little girl, my dad took me to the Coney Island Amusement Park and there was a building decorated just like this one. It had the best ice cream that I had ever tasted."

Tears well up in Maggie's eyes. "Let's order something and just sit for a while."

21

Captain McClellan had been waiting at Jack's desk, which surprised the detective when they entered.

"While you two were frolicking around enjoying yourselves, Barry called. You'll be interested to hear what he has to say. I hope the job isn't interfering with your social lives."

"I guess police captains are the same everywhere," Maggie says to Jack. "They're all ball-busters."

"I heard that!" Captain McClellan says as he leaves the MCU office.

Maggie's mind keeps drifting between the reports and pictures that were on the conference table. She also reflects on her time here in Virginia. This town is getting to her. She begins to understand its appeal.

Jack flips on a TV news station with a remote. His wall-mounted flatscreen has surround sound, with speakers mounted in every corner of the office. Maggie is impressed.

"Must be nice during football season, Jack! You good ol' boys running a betting parlor out of here?"

Jack ignores the comment and turns up the volume. CNN reports the death of Henry Miles. A TV anchor says that the New York medical examiner has ruled the death a homicide. According to unnamed sources, drug cartel leader Tyrone Perkins is a person of interest in the murder of the partner from the Miles and Stratton Law Firm.

"Dammit! Dammit! Dammit to hell! How the hell did they get this information so quickly? How did they find out about Tyrone Perkins so quickly?" Maggie is furious. "This better not have come from Barry or one of my people."

She'll call Barry when she calms down.

Maggie returns to the evidence folders and, again, looks at one of the crime scene photos. This picture is the master bedroom in Janet's suite. On the nightstand were files marked "Tyrone Perkins." The type was small, but legible. If Janet Hastings was here to rest, why bring work with her, and why files? She would have had a laptop.

"Jack, could you come in here? If you go on a vacation, do you take your investigation files with you?"

"No. What did I miss?"

Maggie shows him the photo. "Tell me what you see. What's on the night stand?"

Jack sees a file folder labeled "Tyrone Perkins." He studies the photo more closely.

"Oh, shit! No fuckin' way! This is the master bedroom."

"Yes, but why are you surprised? She was renting the bungalow. Every renter uses that room."

"Maybe, but this isn't the room Janet was staying in. She slept in the smaller room on the Bay side. I remember because I thought that was odd. But that's where all her stuff was placed. I can't believe I missed this!" exclaims Jack.

Jack immediately calls the CSU lab. Stacey Warwick, the senior CSU technician, answers.

"Stacey, I have a question for you?"

"Jack, how did you know I was just getting ready to call you? I have some news for you concerning the evidence we found at the beach bungalow."

"Stacey? Tell me you got prints from the killer!"

"No, but we did get fingerprints in virtually every

room except the master bedroom. Nothing! At first we thought that odd, since most renters would use that room. So we rechecked all of the evidence and print locations."

"Stacey, what about the file folder found in the master bedroom?"

"Jack, here's the big thing: We didn't find any prints on that folder. In fact, her prints were not on anything in the folder, either!"

"Stacey, I could kiss you. Great job!"

"As I said earlier, this didn't make sense so we rechecked everything. We did find a thumbprint of someone else on the back of one of the pages in the file, and it wasn't Janet's. Please don't let this out yet until we find out whom it belongs to. We are researching now. I'll text you as soon as I have something."

22

The news about Henry Miles has legs. CNN keeps the story live throughout the day with updates from Robin Meade, a legal affairs correspondent based in New York. Robin is fairly well-respected for a TV personality. She has a broadcasting degree and had worked as a reporter in Chicago before moving to Atlanta. Cops trust her because she never burns a source. Men also like her looks—a slender, mixed-race woman who can easily pass as a model. She often towers over people she interviews on camera. Off camera, she can be very flirtatious. She was twice married and divorced, both times to cops.

"Today we are reporting on the death of a prominent attorney and senior partner of the Miles and Stratton Law Offices. CNN has learned that Henry Miles was performing his own investigation into one of his partners, who we suspect was Janet Hastings, and her dealings with her clients. Ms. Hastings was murdered just a few days ago on the beach of a small Chesapeake Bay town in Virginia. Sources tell CNN that both deaths are suspected murders and that the cases may be linked."

Meade has a lot of details on the case, information that only police investigators should know about. She reports that Mr. Miles's housekeeper found him the next morning when she arrived at the penthouse. The alarm had not been triggered and he was found lying just inside the door. It appears, Meade says, that Mr. Miles knew his killer and let him into his apartment.

"CNN has also learned that the persons of interest in the Miles murder are international cartel boss Tyrone Perkins and Attorney Janet Hastings. Janet Hastings was well-known throughout New York for her notorious clients, including Tyrone Perkins. According to our sources, she had not been seen since two days before Henry Miles' death. Sources say that she was on vacation at an undisclosed location."

23

Captain McClellan enters Jack's office and sees the two detectives sitting at the conference table, staring at a photograph.

"What is going on? This is the second time today you came up here without being asked," Jack says.

"Detectives, please follow me to my office."

Jack notices that all the blinds on the glass walls that face the squad room in the captain's office are closed. Weird, he thinks. He taps Maggie's shoulder and points toward the closed blinds. Maggie is stunned. She had seen this same tactic at her office in New York and she knew it wasn't going to be good.

Maggie enters after Captain McClellan and sees the person sitting on the sofa.

"Holy shit! Mr. Tyrone Perkins!"

Tyrone ignores Maggie's outburst. He stands and approaches with hand extended. Jack steps between them and introduces himself.

Tyrone and Captain McClellan sit next to each other on the sofa. Maggie takes a seat directly across from Tyrone. Jack glances around the squad room prior to shutting the door. He figures that if this individual is actually Tyrone Perkins he must have "associates" or lawyers lingering somewhere close. Tyrone speaks first.

"Detectives, I am aware of your investigation. I was at my home, in Rio de Janeiro, when I was informed of the two deaths. I was also informed that you, Detective Williams, had been sent here to Virginia to work with the local police department on Ms. Hastings's murder. Janet and I had become very close and it saddens me to lose her like this. Before you ask, our relationship was only business. As soon as I was informed, I contacted my pilot and told him to fly me directly here and not New York."

"Detective Williams, may I call you Maggie?"

She nods.

"Fortunately, there's a private airstrip within fifteen miles of here that is large enough to handle a private jet. Anyway, I have heard that you think that I, either directly or indirectly, may be responsible for at least one or both of these crimes. I assure you that I am not. I was in Rio."

He continues, "I can also assure you that no one from any of my organizations has been involved with these murders. I'll make any one of my people available. Janet was dear to me, detectives. I want her killer caught."

Maggie has never seen someone so notorious offer to help with a police investigation. Just as Maggie is going to ask Tyrone a question, the captain's phone rings. The voice asks for Maggie.

"This is Barry. We have some news for you and Jack."

"Barry, I am in Captain McClellan's office. Can I call you back? I have some news for you also."

"Sorry, Maggie, I know who is in the room with you, so just listen. Captain Reynolds is with me and wants to talk on the speaker phone so we can all hear."

Captain Reynolds comes on the line and says, "I guess you are all wondering why Mr. Perkins is in the room. Or better yet, how I knew that he was there? I am sure Mr. Perkins has already briefed you on his whereabouts during the unfortunate circumstances over the past few days. Mr. Perkins and I had a conversation while he was on his plane to Virginia. Barry has briefed me on their investigations and has so far cleared Mr. Perkins of any wrongdoing at the present time. Mr. Perkins, we thank you for your concern and any assistance that you may provide. We were informed of another situation of interest to you as well. While you were flying into Onancock, there was an attack on Matthew Brenner. He was not hurt, but his rented limo will require some bodywork since it took two shots. We think this attack was to make it appear that you, Mr. Perkins, or one of Mr. Brenner's associates, perpetrated these crimes."

This news is a shock, even to Tyrone.

Captain Reynolds continues: "Mr. Perkins, did you know Henry Miles, Stanley Stratton, his protégé, Julius Wainwright, or his secretary, before Janet brought you and your accounts into the firm of Miles and Stratton?"

Tyrone scans the room for all of the participants and then answers, "One of the law firm associates, I do not remember who, had represented one of my local New York businesses. But that was about a year before

I met Janet. Mr. Stratton and I did meet once at a party in Paris. If I recall, it was a passing meet and greet, and that was it. I personally have not had any contact with him since. In fact, once Janet brought my accounts to the firm, I still had no contact with them. I left that up to Janet. I only signed the paperwork as required. One of my New York executives, Matthew Brenner, met with Janet and the partners for the final signing. I was in the meeting via a video teleconferencing call from my yacht in Rio."

Tyrone knows that he can't divulge his contacts in New York, especially with Captain Reynolds. He had met Stanley Stratton once before when he was in England for an Oxford University alumni party.

Barry thanks Mr. Perkins for his answer and says that Captain McClellan needs to speak with him privately. Captain McClellan stands and Tyrone follows him to a conference room. Jack sees a couple of silhouettes waiting inside the room. Perkins didn't show up alone.

24

As Matthew Brenner exits his limo at the New York office of New England Foods, two shots strike the top of the limo. His security team hustles him into the building. The shooter, perched on the roof of a building across the street, wants to scare him, not kill him.

The shooter's confidence level is high. He knew that Tyrone's highest executive would be returning to his New York corporate office this week. He carefully planned his attack and escape. The Bank of America building directly across has a helicopter landing pad on its roof and a restaurant a floor below, making for easy access. The Perkins Building, which houses the New

England Foods corporate office, has valet parking for its executives at the building's entrance. Tyrone Perkins is such an arrogant bastard that he had renamed the building.

The shooter snickers with contempt as he scopes in the limo roof. If he wanted Brenner dead he could do so easily. He had practiced with the rifle and scope at longer distances and could pierce the center of a paper target with ease. He had also practiced quickly detaching the barrel and gunstock so that the weapon would fit into a briefcase.

He laughed at the security team ducking and then scrambling to get Matthew out of harm's way. The attempt on Brenner would be a distraction, a ploy to make it appear that Perkins and his executives were linked to the other murders. The cops would certainly explore this. The more confusion, the better.

The shooter slips down a utility stairway used by workers and into a service hallway behind the restaurant kitchen. Briefcase in hand, wearing a plain brown suit, he blends with the salesmen, brokers, and other office workers who frequent the bank building restaurant. He knows the layout of the building well because he has clients here. Hopefully, he won't be recognized today.

As he steps onto the elevator he feels invincible, even brilliant. Fuck Janet Hastings! Fuck the law firm! I'll show them justice. Fuck that hoodlum Perkins and the thieves who work for him. I should be the one with limo service, living in a penthouse, attending board meetings on yachts.

25

Maggie is visibly pissed after Tyrone leaves the meeting with the captain. Jack breaks the silence.

"Barry, they're gone and the door is shut. You had better say something quickly or Maggie is coming through the phone to strangle you."

Barry laughs and says, "I was waiting for her to cool down. I know I can't see her, but I bet she is about ready to explode."

"Don't patronize me, asshole. Just tell me what in the hell is going on."

Barry tells Maggie that she needs to return to New York. The case is moving fast. The district attorney

wants a briefing and Captain Reynolds scheduled a
meeting for tomorrow. "Jack, have a bag packed and
be ready to join Maggie within the hour. We need you
here, too.

"Jack, there are some jurisdictional issues that
your captain, our captain and the two district attorneys
have been discussing since this morning. Your captain
has already agreed to send you here. Maggie, your hotel has already been informed that you will be checking
out."

Jack looks at Maggie in disbelief. "I knew you New
York pricks would take over my case."

"Not necessarily," Barry returns.

"Jack, you heard Barry. Get your ass moving, we
have a trip to take," Maggie snaps back. "This is a big-
league case, Jack. Just accept it. You can ride with me."

Captain McClellan and Tyrone Perkins open the
door to the office. He tells Jack and Maggie to sit back
down.

"OK, now that you two are up to speed on the New
York side of the investigation, there is one more twist
that you need to know. Mr. Perkins has graciously of-
fered to fly both of you to New York today. He was
heading there once we were finished here anyway.
This is awkward but necessary. Maggie, Mr. Perkins

will also have a driver take your car back to New York. Now, you two have a plane to catch, so get your files together and bags packed and be back here in an hour. There will be a car waiting to take you to the airstrip. Jack, ensure all the evidence that you take to New York is properly sealed and stays in your possession."

Approximately one hour after they leave, both of the detectives return to the precinct with bags packed. A car takes them to the airfield.

The only so-called private plane Jack has been a passenger on belonged to the U.S. Navy when he was in the Marines. It was a Navy C130 cargo plane. What a difference. Tyrone's plane is definitely not a C130, with its heated, plush leather seats, headphones, a sixty inch flat-screen TV, a small fridge, and all the first class accommodations one could want. The cockpit is separated by a glass partition which slides open, nothing like the double metal doors on commercial aircraft.

Maggie pretends she is unimpressed, calling the plane an expensive taxi. She remains suspicious and wants Tyrone to know it. She's not some impressionable college girl or a sycophant. She's an NYPD detective who's seen plenty of big shots.

"So, how long before we can get off this thing, Mr. Perkins?"

"An hour, Maggie, and please call me Tyrone."

"I appreciate your generosity. I'd prefer to keep this formal," she says.

Jack clearly seems more impressed, so Tyrone turns his attention to the Virginia detective. He tells Jack it's a 2005 Gulf Stream G350. It's actually a jet that cruises at 450 miles per hour.

Everyone quiets down as the plane zips down the runway and starts its ascent. Tyrone climbs into the cockpit into the co-pilot chair and slides the door behind him.

"Maggie, you need to relax," Jack says. "Enjoy the ride."

She says nothing, staring out the window as Onancock fades below.

"Maybe this will cheer you up. Stacey told me that she found a fingerprint on one of the sheets of paper in the folder that was placed on the nightstand."

"Thanks for telling Jack. What else are you holding back? I thought we were partners."

"OK! OK! I apologize. It's a thumbprint on the back of one of the pages. Stacey said that all the others seem to have been handled with gloves or wiped clean somehow."

"Do you know who that print belongs to?" asks

Maggie.

"Yes, I received a text message just before we entered the plane."

"Well? Are you going to tell me, who?"

Just as Jack is about to give her the name, Tyrone slides the cockpit door open and sits across from his guests. He offers them a drink. "I don't drink while I am on the job," Maggie says. Jack looks at Tyrone and just shrugs.

"I guess every party has a pooper," Jack says.

26

When the pilot signals that it is OK to become more comfortable, Tyrone provides complimentary soft drinks to Jack and Maggie. The two notice a door in the back of the cab.

"You want to see it," Tyrone asks. "It's an office."

The Gulfstream G350 was originally designed for eight passengers, but to make room for an office half of the seats had to be removed. The remaining seats face each other to allow passengers to talk during the flight.

The office is cramped but functional. It has a desk, large-screen TV, a computer, and a bed that doubles as a couch. "This is great for long flights," he says of the bed.

Back in the main cabin, Tyrone relaxes, sips on a bottle of spring water, and talks about his family, home in Rio, and his love for fishing. Planes, he says, are a necessary evil. He never flies commercial, he says.

What a charmer, Maggie thinks. Well-educated and well-spoken. I'm sure lots of people are fooled. Jack seems to be.

Jack chats with Tyrone about their mutual love for the big game fish. Jack tells about some large yellow fin tuna he has landed in the Gulf Stream off of the Outer Banks of North Carolina; he talks about the resurgence of striped bass in the Chesapeake Bay.

"Jack, when this mess is over I need to take you fishing on my yacht. I call her the 'Big Deal.'"

Tyrone tells Jack a couple of fish stories of his own. Off of the coast of Australia he hooked a great white shark that took Tyrone and a boat mate four and a half hours to land. It measured fourteen feet in length and weighed about thirty-eight-hundred pounds.

Jack's yellow fin tuna stories now seemed so pedestrian.

"I really prefer the Bluefin off the coast where I live in Rio. They run four to six feet and go around four hundred pounds. They aren't as big as the great whites, but they're fierce."

"Yeah, they don't usually run that large in the Gulf Stream, but there are some nice ones out there."

Tyrone reiterates his invitation for Jack to join him in Rio.

Tyrone turns his attention toward Maggie, who seems unimpressed.

"Detective Williams, do you enjoy the outdoors much?"

"Mr. Perkins, let's keep this professional, OK?"

"Well then, do you have any professional things you'd like to discuss?"

"What actually are your dealings with the Miles and Stratton Law Office?" she asks.

"All of my interactions with the Miles and Stratton Law Offices have been all legal and legitimate. Janet made it clear that she and her firm would not break any laws or condone illegal activities. In fact, that's stated in the retainer contract I have with the firm."

Tyrone anticipates Maggie's next question. Why pick Janet as his lawyer?

Tyrone says he learned about Janet from his executives in New York who were impressed with her tough but intelligent demeanor. She was attractive and sharp. She was deferential but honest. Tyrone and his executives wanted someone young who they could develop a long-term relationship with. They wanted someone based in New York with a powerful firm to draw on when needed.

The pilot summons Tyrone to the cockpit. Maggie contemplates what Tyrone has said here and in Captain McClellan's office back in Onancock. As much as she hates to admit it, she is starting to have the same feelings about Tyrone as her partner, Barry. Perkins may, in fact, have become a pawn in an elaborate scheme to shift blame from the firm, or someone in the firm, to a person of his power and notoriety.

Barry and the Onancock evidence technician, Stacey, had uncovered enough evidence to move the investigation in a different direction. The fingerprint Jack had mentioned would be the key.

The pilot signals that they are on final approach to LaGuardia. Tyrone returns to the passenger cabin and thanks the two detectives. A car is waiting at the airport to give them a ride to the Manhattan precinct, he says. Tyrone goes into his office, closes the door, calls Matthew Brenner.

"Matthew, we are on final approach to LaGuardia. I need you to meet me in my private hangar. No rush, because I need to make sure the two detectives are out of sight before I have the pilot move the aircraft."

"Two detectives? You have two detectives onboard your aircraft? Are you under arrest?" asks Matthew.

"No, no handcuffs, just questions. I want them to get the asshole who took potshots at you."

27

Jack and Maggie climb into the waiting car. Maggie tells the driver she needs to go home before heading to the precinct.

The driver helps carry Jack's and Maggie's bags to her second-floor apartment. A small sitting area with a sea-green sofa fills the middle of the room with its back toward the only window. Two potted plants sit on the bench beneath the window.

The small kitchen has an apartment-size refrigerator, microwave, and stove. No dishes on the countertops or in the sink. No dishwasher, either. Maggie must eat out a lot, Jack thinks. Maggie heads toward her bedroom. Jack notices a spare bedroom next to it.

Maggie emerges looking as beautiful as ever. Her clothes are more formal now, probably because she's heading into work, he thinks.

"Jack, this is your room while you are here," Maggie says, pointing to the spare. "There is a bathroom just across the hall with a tub and shower combo. If you would like to freshen up, go ahead. We have time."

"Are you sure this is OK? I can stay at a hotel."

"Yes, Jack. It is OK, now go get freshened up. We need to go to the precinct before it gets too late."

28

When Maggie and Jack enter the squad room, Maggie's team members shout, "How-dy! Welcome to New York City!" They all attempted a Southern drawl. Maggie is embarrassed.

One of the female detectives stops in front of Jack, slowly running her eyes from his head to his feet.

"Your Southern boy is hot, Maggie."

Cops in the squad room roar with laughter.

"Nice group of people you work with here, Maggie," Jacks says in a soft voice. "I can see they really missed you."

Barry watches from the door entrance to the break

room, laughing with the rest of the crowd.

"Maggie. We missed you! Can't you tell? By the way, did you enjoy the flight?" he smirks. "They didn't lose your baggage, did they? Jack, you should have Maggie book your return flight. Isn't that right, Maggie?"

"Screw you, Barry," Maggie says. "You should be working instead of sitting around planning stupid stunts to bust my balls."

Barry just smiles at Jack. "Life in the big city," he says.

"OK, enough of that, I have everything set up in the conference room. Jack, you can put your evidence box in there also." All three detectives stroll to the conference room to consolidate and sort all of their evidence from both of the recent murders, as well as the evidence from Maggie's earlier case.

Fifteen minutes later, Assistant District Attorney Jessica Lawrence and Captain Reynolds enter the conference room. Jessica starts speaking immediately while lowering herself into a chair.

"Good afternoon, detectives. I have been on the phone with the Virginia State Attorney General's office. They have agreed to allow New York to arrest and prosecute the individual, or individuals, responsible for the murder of Janet Hastings and Henry Miles, first and foremost. New York will maintain jurisdiction over the attempt on Matthew Brenner. They have also agreed that if a conviction cannot be obtained in New York, they will hold arrest warrants and extradition papers for the person, or persons, involved with the murder in Virginia. Detective Sinclair, I personally want to thank you for being part of this investigation. And I hope you enjoy your stay in our little town."

Jack nods and thanks her.

"Jack, could you break out the evidence from Virginia? Barry, let's lay out the evidence from here and correlate all of it for Jessica," Maggie says. She's back in her element now and is getting excited again.

"Jack, hand me the bedroom pictures that the crime scene unit took." Jack searches the boxes, finds the photos, and hands them to Maggie who passes the first picture to Jessica.

"Tell me what you see in this picture?"

Jessica is surprised to be put on the spot, but plays along.

"There's a file folder on the nightstand; this room must be where Janet slept."

"That is what we all thought at first," says Maggie. " Now look at these pictures."

Jessica studies the next three pictures handed to her by Maggie.

"These pictures show clothing on a chair, and a robe on a bathroom door. They appear to be a guest-room. What is significant about these pictures?" Maggie asks.

"This bedroom, the guest room, is the one that Janet occupied. The CSU team did not find any DNA, prints or any other evidence in the master bedroom that would have come from her. They did get plenty of evidence that she had occupied the guestroom. The guestroom had a French door that opened toward the beach. Why the file was on the master bedroom night-stand was a mystery at first. We think the files may have been hastily placed on there as a set up. Why would Janet have taken work files on a vacation? And to leave this material lying around! It didn't make sense."

Maggie continues, "The files only contained basic information about her client, Tyrone Perkins. There really doesn't seem to be anything in them that needed review."

"Who would have the resources to manufacture a fake folder and deliver it to where Janet was spending her vacation? Who would also know her vacation plans?" Jack interjects.

"So, what are you saying?" asks Jessica "You thinking that it's someone from her firm?"

"At first, I was under the impression that Tyrone Perkins, or one of his associates, was involved. On our flight from Virginia to New York, I asked him if he knew Janet's vacation plans. He said he hadn't heard from Janet in a few days and vaguely remembered her mentioning a vacation. He didn't know she was in Virginia until he heard of her death."

Maggie says she wants to interview members of the law firm and she'll need search warrants. Jessica reaches into her bag and tosses the warrants on the table in front of Maggie.

"One step ahead of you," she says. "I was waiting for you to ask. We'll have another set for tomorrow. By the way, there is one there that your team needs to execute today."

Maggie looks surprised. "What other warrants will I need? Who are we serving today?"

"Ask one of those two gents over there."

Jack and Barry look at each other with smirks. They look back at Maggie and see the red returning to her face.

"Barry. Jack. What is she talking about?" Maggie asks angrily.

"I'm sorry Maggie, but I tried to tell you on the plane just before Tyrone came out of his office."

"The thumbprint that Stacey found on one of the pages in the folder turns out to be Mr. Stratton's secretary's."

"Jack texted Barry with the information while you were on the plane. Barry called me and added a request for her home and her office area. The home is for today and the office area will be in tomorrow's set," Jessica says.

Barry then chimes in: "Maggie, we don't believe she is the killer, but she may be involved, or at least lead us to him. After your interview today, I am sure you will have enough evidence to confirm my suspicions."

Maggie addresses Jessica, "I am going to do a preliminary interview with the other remaining law firm partner today. Then if everything goes as planned, we can activate the arrest warrants tomorrow. I'll call you when we're finished."

Maggie looks at Jack and says, "Let's go and I am driving."

29

Jack's glad he's not driving his Jag in this crazy city.

"Where are we going?"

"To Miles and Stratton on Wall Street. We are going to interview Mr. Stratton."

Jack sees the Charging Bull statue in front of the New York Stock Exchange. He has read that the statue symbolizes aggressive financial optimism and prosperity. With all of the struggles of the Wall Street financial institutions lately, people still flock to the statue as if it is an Athenian god. A group of Asian visitors huddle around the Bull and snap pictures with their digital cameras.

The Miles and Stratton Law Office resides in one of the most beautiful buildings in the Wall Street district and directly across from the Exchange. Maggie is impressed by the massive reception area. It's larger than her apartment. The thirty-foot ceilings are adorned with old- world paintings and a large, crystal chandelier directly over an eight-foot diameter "M & S" lettering in the center of the marbled reception-area floor.

"Now we know where my money goes!" says Jack.

As the two detectives approach the receptionist, they are greeted with a huge smile and a cheerful personality. Jack smiles. Maggie gruffly asks to see Stanley Stratton.

"Do you have an appointment with Mr. Stratton?"

"No, but I am sure he will see us," says Maggie as she flashes her badge.

Within a few minutes a young man in his early thirties enters the lobby and greets the detectives. He introduces himself as Julius Wainwright, Mr. Stratton's protégé. Julius has a short fresh haircut and manicured nails and wears a pressed black pinstripe suit and alligator shoes. Jack could pay two month's rent for the price of the outfit.

The three of them wait outside an office with eight-foot double mahogany doors and expensive gold-plated door handles. Jack notices that the secretary is not at her desk.

"Where is Mr. Stratton's secretary?" Jack asks.

"Mr. Stratton gave her the day off today."

Julius barely touches the large mahogany doors, which slowly and evenly spread. The doors have a pneumatic mechanism that opens them with the slightest nudge.

Stanley Stratton's office has three separate sitting areas. On the right is an informal area, with a coffee table and two plush chairs facing a black elephant-skin sofa with its back to a huge window. On the left is a circular conference table made from the same mahogany as the doors. There are thirteen chairs. The one at the head of the table is slightly larger and taller.

Looks like King Arthur Syndrome, thinks Jack.

Stanley Stratton's desk sits in the middle, directly opposite the double doors. His desk and the two wing-back chairs facing the desk make up the third section of his office. The desk is large and ornate, with carved lion's feet and inlays. It must be for show, Jack thinks, because there is nothing on it but a picture frame, a fancy pen, and an iPad next to a gold-plated telephone.

Julius asks the detectives to take a seat at the circular conference table. Jack wonders if "Sir Julius" will join them. Within a couple of minutes, a side door opens and Stanley Stratton enters, strutting with shoulders back and hand extended. He takes the "throne" at the head of the "Round Table".

"Good afternoon, detectives. I understand you have some questions for me. How may I assist you today?"

"Mr. Stratton, I am Detective Maggie Williams and this is Detective Jack Sinclair. We are here investigating the untimely demise of your partners, Henry Miles and Janet Hastings. We would like for you to tell us what you can about Ms. Hastings and your longtime partner Mr. Miles. Did they have anything in common other than being partners?"

"Detective, you know as well as I do that I can only provide you information that resides outside the confines of our company's confidentiality rules."

"Yes, I know," says Maggie, "but we are not asking for anything concerning the firm's clients. We're interested in their personal and work relations. I was hoping to keep this informal and to avoid intervention with subpoenas."

"Again, detective, I must insist that I cannot share

information that touches on any client. I am certain you and the district attorney know this. I will tell you that I was out of the country when these senseless events happened. I can also state that I do not believe that Miles or Janet shared client information. She had just been promoted to partnership prior to her vacation. We can represent each other's clients, as a firm, of course, if needed, but we only get involved at the lead attorney's request."

Maggie presses for more.

"Mr. Stratton, I am certain you're aware by now that your partner, Mr. Miles, had been investigating Janet and her relationship with her main client Tyrone Perkins. It's been reported in the media and is, in fact, true."

Julius interrupts: "I don't believe Mr. Miles had ever met Mr. Perkins until the signing of the contract with the firm. So why would he investigate Mr. Perkins?"

Maggie continues: "I am also certain you're aware of the Interpol investigations into Ms. Hastings and her client, correct? Mr. Stratton, did you know Tyrone Perkins before Janet brought his account to your firm?"

"I knew of him only as a friend to one of our clients, but not personally. I was introduced to him at a party hosted by one of our clients. That was the first and only time that I met him until Janet brought him into our firm."

"Mr. Wainwright, have you ever met Tyrone Perkins? Did you have knowledge of Mr. Miles' investigation as well?"

"I do not believe I have met Mr. Perkins. My answer is no."

Jack is good at reading people and suspects Julius knows more.

"Mr. Wainwright, the receptionist told us that you were also out of the city when Janet was murdered. Where were you?"

"In New Jersey, meeting with a client who is ill and can't travel."

Maggie doesn't remember the receptionist saying anything about Julius. What a ploy!

After a few more minutes and a couple of more questions, Stratton gestures toward the doors. "Officers, I believe I was very cooperative with your questions. I wish you both a great day." He nods to Julius who immediately rises from his chair to escort the detectives out. Stanley remains seated.

Once outside the building, Maggie turns and says, "They definitely avoided most of our questions.

You would think that with two partners dead, Stratton would want to cooperate to make sure he's not next."

Jack replies with a nod and then says, "That other guy is creepy. His head was halfway up Stanley's ass."

30

By the time they return to the precinct, Barry, Jessica, and Captain Reynolds have left for the day. There are only a few team members sitting at their desks finishing up phone calls. Maggie and Jack return to the conference room to work their puzzle.

"My spider senses were tingling once I saw the secretary not there. If you had a secretary, would you send her home if you were in the office? I wouldn't," says Jack.

"I wouldn't unless there was someone filling in," Maggie says. "And I think Stratton's lap boy was lying about being in Jersey with a client. That was a pretty tricky move, Jack, telling him the receptionist said he was out of town. He took the bait all the way."

"I think we should look at him more closely," Jack says. "I think that Julius is the one involved with the secretary. I keep thinking about that fingerprint in the Perkins file. I hope Barry finds something interesting with the warrant at the secretary's house today. It sure would help when we execute those other search warrants in the morning."

Maggie goes to her desk in the squad room and logs onto her computer to search a database of 9mm gun owners in the city. Jack follows and strolls around her desk.

"Nice digs here Maggie. You must have a good ten square feet of space. Lots of privacy," he says sarcastically

"Don't be an ass Jack. You had to go to friggin' Onancock to get an office."

Televisions in the squad room are dialed to a local news station. A special bulletin interrupts the current broadcast. Jack hears the name Matthew Brenner and nudges Maggie.

"Early this week, the CEO of New England Foods was the target of a shooting as he was leaving his limo and entering his New York corporate office. He was not harmed. The security detail stated that there had only been two shots and that both hit the top of the limo. The NYPD has stated that there are no suspects at this current time."

Why only two shots in the roof? Very odd! Jack thinks.

A few minutes later, Maggie motions for Jack to look at her computer screen.

Jack pulls up a chair and sits next to her. Maggie points to her find, turns to look at Jack, and then spontaneously kisses him. Both seem surprised. Maggie smiles and scans the squad room. Thankfully, no one saw what just happened.

"Jack, I think it is time to call Jessica."

Maggie dials the phone and spends the next few minutes explaining to the assistant district attorney what she needs and who, and where, and what time she wants warrants to be served.

Jack re-enters the conference room and she follows him. She's getting flush as her heart pounds. She wants him inside of her now. She grabs Jack again and kicks the conference door shut. They embrace, kiss, and press hard against each other.

"You ready to leave for the night," Jack asks.

"Let's go home," she says.

31

By the time they arrive home, Maggie's ripe passion has cooled. The awkwardness sets in.

"If you don't mind, I am going to hit the shower. If you want to order a pizza, I'll pay."

He removes a couple of twenties from his wallet, lays them on the table in the kitchen area, and heads for the shower. Showered and dressed casually, he emerges from the spare bedroom in a T-shirt and shorts. He smells pizza and heads toward it.

Maggie is lying on the sofa dressed in a small, red babydoll negligee.

"Better than a bikini, much better!" he says staring at her.

Maggie motions for Jack to join her on the sofa.

She tells him the pizza can wait.

Jack lifts her into his strong arms, planting a passionate kiss on her lips. Their hot tongues explore each other's mouthes. He carries her to the spare room and gently places her on "his" bed. It's time for some Southern hospitality.

32

May in New York can be fairly cool. Late spring is known for small pop-up showers that last from a few minutes to a few hours. Today, the sun is shining; no rain is forecasted.

Jack awakes to the smell of fresh coffee brewing. He's naked, refreshed, and content. A robe is draped at the foot of the bed.

As Jack dons the robe and enters the living area, Maggie is standing next to the kitchen counter pouring two cups of coffee. She also wears a robe. She looks gorgeous. Jack wants her again. He walks up to her and spins her to face him.

"You're so beautiful." He presses against her and hardens. She groans, but then gently pushes away.

"As much as I would love to continue this, we have some work to do today. Enjoy your coffee while I hit the shower. I think you might want to hit the shower too." Maggie smiles and pats Jack's ass as she walks past him.

Jack takes a couple of sips from his coffee cup, places it on the cabinet and heads for the shower; but this time it's not "his" shower.

33

Maggie and Jack arrive at the conference room at nine to review their evidence and set strategy for the day's activity.

"Late start today, huh!" Barry smiles as they enter the room. This is unlike Maggie; she is always at the precinct by seven o'clock.

Maggie ignores the comment and calls Jessica. "You coming with us today?"

"Sure, on the way, be there in twenty," Jessica responds. After her conversation with Maggie last night, she isn't going to miss this.

Barry gathers two other team leaders into the

conference room who have been waiting for Maggie and Jack. She explains what she and Jack discovered on the computer last night and what the teams should concentrate on finding.

"How did you put the pieces together?" Barry asks.

"I didn't, Jack did! After we left the interview last evening, he told me about his 'spider senses' and how they were tingling."

"That's right. I'm an insect," Jack quips, "and Maggie is the bloodhound."

"So, you think she's a dog?" Barry laughs.

"Enough, little boys," Maggie barks. "I was doing research on the registered owners of a 9mm here in the city last night. We have the name of someone at the firm, but it's not Perkins or his people."

"During my research last night, a news report of an attack on Matthew Brenner was being broadcasted on WNBC. The attack took place as Tyrone Perkins was in flight to Virginia. That and no link to the gun means Tyrone is not our guy," Maggie says.

Maggie reviews the search and arrest plan with the others.

"Jack, Barry, Jessica and I will go to the law firm. The other teams will execute the warrants at the home of the suspect and at the firm after we corral everyone.

Team leaders, ensure you stay in contact with each other all the time. Text me, Jack or Barry, with your findings immediately. We'll hold everyone's attention long enough for you to execute the warrants."

Fifteen minutes later, Jessica Lawrence walks into the squad room with all the necessary search warrants in hand and hands them to Maggie.

"Let's roll."

34

The law firm receptionist recognizes Jack and Maggie. "I assume you want to speak with Mr. Stratton again," she says in a shrill voice. "I assume these officers are with you."

Before she can dial, Maggie reaches over the desk and takes the handset from her and places it back on the large, black intercom telephone set.

"We are here not only to see Mr. Stratton, but also his entire staff. Please call Julius Wainwright and have him contact Mr. Stratton, his entire staff. and have them meet us in Mr. Stratton's office. Do not call Mr. Stratton."

Jack whispers to Barry, "Maggie seems to enjoy this."

"Her dad was a cop and she had three brothers. She can be a hard ass."

The receptionist follows Maggie's instructions and leads the entourage to Mr. Stratton's office. Maggie takes a seat at the huge round table. Jack and Barry stand next to the entrance.

"King Arthur and his knights!" Jack whispers to Barry. "By the way, did you get lucky with the search yesterday?"

"Yes, I should be getting a text this morning. I hope it arrives when we are here. Maggie will be elated," Barry whispers.

The legal staff begins trickling in. Some join Maggie at the table. Others stand along the walls as the room fills. Some of the legal interns have never seen the office before. Jack sees them gazing at the furniture and artwork in awe.

Stanley Stratton and Julius Wainwright arrive last. "Detectives, we are all here as requested. I don't know why you have to be so dramatic. You're disrupting the work of this firm." Stanley takes his regular seat at the table and motions with his hand for Maggie to begin.

"Mr. Stratton, as you know, I am Detective Maggie Williams. You have met Detective Jack Sinclair. What I didn't tell you before is that he is from the major crime unit in Onancock, a small town on Virginia's Eastern Shore. This is Jessica Lawrence, assistant district attorney for New York, and Detective Barry Carter, my partner."

Without pausing, she says, "Detective Sinclair is here because Janet Hastings was killed while vacationing in Onancock. She was found shot twice on the beach. We believe that a killer hid in the sand dunes and stalked Ms. Hastings. We also believe that he gained access to Ms. Hastings's bungalow from the back door that was left unlocked and planted some incriminating evidence meant to lead our investigation toward an obvious suspect."

Maggie continues: "As Janet slept silently, her attacker walked quietly and methodically through the sandy beach and put two bullets into her body. Either shot would have killed her. Now what perplexed us all was the untimely and unfortunate death of Henry Miles, your co-founder. We believe he was killed by the same person. We have evidence linking their deaths."

"We also believe that the same person fired shots at Matthew Brenner, the New York executive who works for Tyrone Perkins. I believe most of your staff knows Ms. Hastings represented both Mr. Perkins and Mr. Brenner."

Some of the staff members gasp. Others look at each other in disbelief. The deaths are connected to the firm.

The two detectives start moving toward the office doors to block anyone from leaving. Jack covers the main entrance and Barry shifts toward the door that Stanley and Julius entered earlier. Barry receives a text message, apologizes for interrupting, and shows it to Maggie and Jessica. Without changing her expression, Maggie begins again.

"Now we know that this firm has increased its clientele and income since Janet joined. We also know that one of your clients had been a person of interest in all of these cases. Let me be clear: Tyrone Perkins is not a suspect and neither is anyone who works directly for him. We believe the murderer is in this room."

All eyes turn to Stanley Stratton. All, that is, except one set.

Stanley starts to stand, but Maggie stands quicker and places a hand on his shoulder and forces him back into his seat.

"Detective Williams, I have had about enough of

this. Unless you have an arrest warrant, this meeting is over. You and your detectives need to gather yourselves and leave immediately."

Jessica steps up and firmly says, "Mr. Stratton, if you would, please indulge Detective Williams. This will only take a few more minutes."

She nods and Maggie continues.

"In every case, there was a slip-up by the perpetrator. Everyone makes a mistake. The biggest mistakes occur when one tries to blame someone else. In this case, the one piece of evidence that gave it away was initially seen as a coincidence.

"The perpetrator forgot that Janet went to Virginia for a vacation to get away from her work and this firm. There was no reason for her to have work files with her and the paperwork inside them was routine information on her client, Tyrone Perkins. The files were also left in a bedroom that she didn't use."

Maggie lays the picture of the file on the nightstand in front of Mr. Stratton.

She continues, "We also found a thumbprint on the back of one of the pages in the folder. You may think this is normal, but there were no other fingerprints on any other pages or on the folder itself. That print belongs to a person with access to all the firm's

BASCOM WILSON 159

files. We believe the killer was also angry about Janet making partner, especially when he, or she, was removed from contingency.

"This individual made more slip-ups. Another was the fake attack on Matthew Brenner. It was a thinly-veiled diversion. But seriously, two shots in the roof of a limo when the target is in plain sight!

"Mr. Stratton, while you were out of the country, your secretary, who has been missing for a couple of days now, was working with another person in your firm. The thumbprint on the page belongs to her. Yesterday, we executed a search warrant at her home and today we are currently executing a warrant on her accomplice's home."

The text message Barry showed earlier to Maggie confirmed her suspicion. Stratton's secretary is dead.

Maggie continues, "Mr. Stratton, your secretary was not at home grieving the loss of Mr. Miles or Ms. Hastings. She is, in fact, dead. Our officers found her yesterday. She had been shot twice and in the same manner as Ms. Hastings."

Barry walks over to Maggie and shows her another text message. Stanley Stratton sits slumped, silent, and dumbfounded.

"We have confirmed that the weapon is the same

caliber used on Ms. Hastings."

The staff members at the table and along the walls start to mumble among themselves. They are trying to figure out who did the murders before Detective Williams says the name. Jessica jumps in:

"Mr. Stratton, I am here to inform you that the murder suspect is Mr. Julius Wainwright. Mr. Wainwright, you are under arrest."

All eyes shift to Julius. The interns and staff are stunned.

Maggie looks into his eyes and states, "As an attorney, you know your Miranda Rights; but as a precaution to eliminate a future technicality, the detective will read you your rights as they escort you out. Mr. Wainwright, please rise. Detective Carter, escort this man out of this room."

Jack gestures for everyone else to remain.

Barry lifts Julius out of the chair, handcuffs him, and escorts him outside of the room where uniformed officers wait to take him to the precinct.

Jessica asks Mr. Stratton to remain as the rest of the staff members are asked to leave the office.

"Mr. Stratton, Detective Williams and I apologize for dragging this out, but we had to execute the search warrants without the knowledge of your staff. You also needed to know how we reached the decision about Julius Wainwright. I will be prosecuting him. I would also recommend that you and your firm recuse yourself from defending him. He has killed at least four times in the name of your firm."

Jack, Jessica, and Maggie shake Mr. Stratton's hand before departing. As they walk through the lobby, Jack says, "A king and his court!"

Maggie tells Jack that she had hoped to tie Julius to Tyrone. "That bastard is still untouchable," she says.

"Another day," says Jack. "Enjoy this one. We did good!"

35

The investigation teams discovered that Julius had been dating Mr. Stratton's secretary for over a year, hiding it from everyone in the firm. His jealousy of Janet, her clientele, and the eagerness of the senior partners to make her a partner instead of him, sent him over the edge. He felt that his twenty years with the firm as the personal confidante should have made his selection as partner incontestable.

Barry's re-investigation of Maggie's earlier case connected notes to Julius Wainwright also. The case had been pulled from her before she was given the chance to make sense of what she had discovered.

Maggie knew that if she had been given the chance earlier, Julius Wainwright would have been in prison and both Janet and Henry would still be alive. Wainwright had murdered before, for the same reason.

Julius had been with the firm twenty years. He was the personal confidante of both Henry Miles and Stanley Stratton. He had been passed over as partner before. While he was well-regarded, Julius was seen as more of an aide than a gifted lawyer. His client base was small and he didn't drum up much business.

He was, however, well-organized and well-spoken. Stratton often commented to Miles that he thought Julius would have made an excellent executive assistant. Privately, the two men often jokingly referred to him as the 'receptionist'. They wondered if he was gay—he never married and showed up at most firm parties stag.

Julius also served another purpose; he was plugged into office gossip and was quick to share grapevine chatter with Henry and Stanley. Julius saw himself as a gatekeeper to the big bosses, which brought him stature and revere. What he didn't know is that others in the firm saw him for what he is, an ass kisser, a suck-up, a jealous boy trying to get ahead by playing politics instead of busting his butt writing legal briefs and trying cases.

36

Tyrone Perkins returns to his home in Rio. Interpol dropped its cases against him and he's feeling relieved.

The law office of Miles and Stratton changes its name to The Stratton Law Firm of New York. Stanley Stratton has been able to keep nearly all of Henry's and Janet's clients and the law firm is once again booming.

The summer days in New York are hot and humid. Maggie hates the walk from her apartment through the concrete forest to get to her precinct during the summer. Even taking a taxi is excruciating.

She dreams of how it would be back in Virginia on the Chesapeake Bay. Even though it is probably hot there too, the breezes would bring relief. She thinks about two scoops of chocolate pecan from Sally's Ice Cream Parlor.

It has been a couple of months since Jack returned to Virginia. As much as she does not want to admit it, Jack has gotten into her head, and heart. They had one other encounter the night before she drove him to the airport. She wants his lifestyle—she wants him. She has never felt this way about a man. She has never felt that she could leave her life as a NYPD detective, either.

She is torn between two worlds.

37

The arrest of Julius Wainwright made headlines throughout New York. Local Virginia and Maryland stations picked up the story too. Julius was charged with murder and could receive life sentences in New York. In Virginia, he could receive the death penalty. As part of the jurisdictional deal with New York, Virginia's AG office maintained the right to try him for the Hastings murder.

Onancock became its own big city overnight. The publicity showed the town and its beaches, stoking interest among tourists. Jack also became a bit of a star. He was credited for the arrest. He returned to Onancock with complimentary tickets to a Knicks game. He loves watching the Knicks, but hasn't been able to see a game in person.

In the weeks after the arrest, Jack hasn't heard from his NYPD counterparts. It is back to work as usual. Major cases on the Eastern Shore feel mundane, but he loves it. New York wasn't for him, but one of its residents is. He misses Maggie.

He knows she loves her job and the city. He knows she won't give that up to be with him. It's how he feels about his town and job, also.

He struggles with the memory of Maggie. He has never felt this way for a woman. It is driving him crazy. His longlife friend, Dan, encourages him to follow his heart. But what exactly is his heart telling him?

38

The retirement of Captain Brady McClellan of the Onancock Police Department is a big deal in Onancock. It's a small town and therefore any event could be big if planned correctly, especially if it is the retirement of their police captain. A celebration brings family members and friends together as one community for speeches, bands, dancing, and of course, plenty of good food to eat.

Dan and Jack had heard that Captain McClellan's replacement is going to be announced at his retirement ceremony. Jack hopes it will be Dan. He deserves it.

The Eastern Shore Police chief is the guest speaker at Captain McClellan's retirement. During his speech, he mentions the joint cooperation between the NYPD and the OPD in arresting an interstate murderer. The chief is a good politician; he can speak on any subject. As he finishes he asks Captain McClellan to join him at the podium to announce his replacement. Jack looks at Dan and his wife, Nancy, and smiles. This is going to be a bittersweet moment. Good for Dan! If promoted, Dan, his best friend, will now be his boss.

The chief turns the microphone over to Captain McClellan. He starts by saying, "The past few months caused me to think of my future plans. The fish in the Bay have been calling, so I take this time to officially announce my retirement. As my last official duty, I am going to introduce my replacement as the new captain of the Onancock Police Department, Captain Dan Miller."

Dan looks at Jack, who immediately gives his longtime friend a giant bear hug. Dan grabs his wife's hand and leads her to the podium. The entire OPD, as well as the community members in attendance, provide a standing ovation.

"As the new captain of the Onancock OPD, I have been given the permission to hire another detective.

We are expanding our force to not only cover the northern section of the Eastern Shore, but we have been designated as the primary MCU for the entire Eastern Shore; therefore, to assist our now famous Detective Jack Sinclair, I present..."

This stuns Jack; he had no idea. "Now, two detectives!" he quietly says. He stares hard at the podium for his new partner.

From behind the podium in full Virginia OPD dress uniform appears the newest member of the Onancock Police Department—Detective Maggie Williams.

Beach Murder Mysteries

Read more from Köehler Book's Beach Murder Mysteries collection of books. Go to www.beachmurdermysteries.com and orders your book in print from Amazon or Barnes & Noble, and in epub on Kindle, Nook and iBooks.

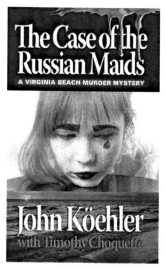

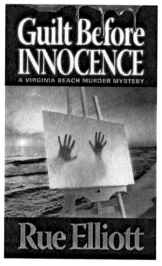

CPSIA information can be obtained at www.ICGtesting.com
Printed in the USA
LVOW052020300712

292200LV00002B/10/P

9 781938 467127